KATJA FROM THE PUNK BAND

SIMON LOGAN

ChiZine Publications

FIRST EDITION

Katja From the Punk Band © 2010 by Simon Logan
Jacket design © 2010 by Erik Mohr
All Rights Reserved.

LIBRARY AND ARCHIVES CANADA CATALOGUING IN PUBLICATION

Logan, Simon, 1977-
          Katja from the punk band / Simon Logan.

ISBN 978-0-9812978-7-3

          I. Title.

PR6112.O33K38 2010   823'.92   C2010-900651-8

CHIZINE PUBLICATIONS
Toronto, Canada
www.chizinepub.com
info@chizinepub.com

Edited by Brett Alexander Savory
Copyedited and proofread by Sandra Kasturi

PART ONE
KATJA FROM THE PUNK BAND

CHAPTER ONE

So she walks in, trying to look cool, trying to look like nothing has happened, like nothing has gone wrong, but it's difficult because she still feels the ghost of the revolver's handle pressed against her palm and the scent of gunpowder in her nostrils.

Her liberty spikes are limp from the rain that battered her as she ran to the diner, her bruise-like makeup streaking her cheeks and angular jaw line. Water is collecting on the translucent plastic tube that sticks out of a hole in the middle of her neck, and dribbles from it as the door swings shut behind her, closing out the smog and the rumble of machinery.

The place is quiet, the usual cases of human debris scattered amongst the booths lingering over bowls of soup or chili. Freya is taking an order from a group of men whose bags litter the floor by their feet. They are roaches, those whose have a permanent stink of peroxide and ammonia, whose job it is to crawl through empty factories and old chimney shafts, scraping out the chemical grime. Freya's face is screwed up from the odour when she turns and notices Katja.

Katja strides past the other woman, flips open the counter hatch and goes through a door into the kitchen beyond.

There is the stench of old fat and new fat, of fried onions and sweat. She grabs a towel from a collection of them hanging from a bare nail spiked into one of the walls and begins to rub her shoulders and arms dry. She is about to reach into the pocket of her combats when the door swings open and Freya walks in. Katja's hand freezes where it is, then finds something else to do. She rubs the short, shaved hair at the sides of her head.

"You okay?" Freya asks. "You're late."

She grabs some bowls from the stack on the preparation counter before her and lifts the lid off of a large black pot that steams when she opens it. Katja's stomach turns at the meaty stench, her hand going to her mouth.

"I'm fine," she replies, taking an apron from the same nail the towel was hanging from.

Freya slops some of the dark mess from the pot into the bowl. Katja dry-heaves again.

"Your arm," Freya says softly, without looking up. "Did he . . . ?"

And it is only then that Katja notices the welt that runs

across her forearm, wrist to elbow, and the small cut at the centre of it. With the realization comes the pain.

"It's nothing," she says distractedly and quickly busies herself putting on her apron so she can turn away from the other waitress. "Things got out of hand at the gig last night."

"I can stay a little bit longer if you need to—"

"No," Katja says and immediately knows she was too harsh. She tongues her lip piercing. "You have to go. Get home. Do you want me to take those?"

Freya shakes her head. "Never mind. I'll do it myself." She pushes her way out into the service area and, once she is gone, Katja looks down at the wound on her arm.

Shit.

She reaches into her pocket and pulls out the vial when she sees Freya putting the bowls of chili down through the service window for the roaches. The vial is about six inches long and mostly translucent save for the frosted watermark that identifies it as coming from Dracyev's chemical labs. Inside it a thin, gold-tinged liquid moves, contained by a jet black rubber stopper. Katja opens a drawer stuffed with old, rusted utensils and places it carefully inside.

Next she hears the *ding* of the entrance bell and her heart rate spikes. She peers through the service window and watches as a pale man with black hair hanging over his eyes enters. He glances around momentarily at the other customers then sits at the counter. He meets Katja's eyes through the opening.

"Be with you in a minute," she tells the man.

She closes the drawer, breathes.

"You getting this one? Because I'm off now," Freya says through the window.

"Sure."

Katja hesitates at the door to the service area, a sudden rush of adrenaline surging through her as if she expects someone else to be waiting for her on the other side. She peers through the window.

There is a lone girl stooped over a bowl of soup, letting the steam wash over her face as she stares down into it. A runaway, most likely.

There is an older couple that don't look at each other while they eat their sandwiches.

There is a couple of truckers sitting by empty bowls and coffee cups, playing some sort of card game with one another. One of them looks up and catches Katja's eye, smiles as he goes back to the cards.

She thinks *what was he smiling at?*

She thinks *was he smiling at me?*

She thinks *why was he smiling at me? Does he know?*

Shit. Shit. Shit.

"Hey."

And it's Freya, scowling at her through the service opening.

"What the fuck is up with you? Are you going to get to work or not?"

Katja tongues her lip piercing, pushes one of her flopping liberty spikes away from the back of her neck. It feels like a dead snake, like the arm of a lecherous uncle.

"I'm washing my hands."

This is what she says to Freya as the other woman comes into the kitchen and drops her apron, pulls on her jacket.

She turns on the tap of one of the sinks and rinses her hands once, twice, then dries them off on the same towel she used on herself earlier. The fabric has become sticky with clots of the egg whites she uses to stiffen her spikes.

"See you tomorrow," Freya says as she pokes a cigarette into her mouth and leaves through the heavy steel door at the back entrance. Katja stares at it for several moments after the woman is gone, considering it.

In the end she goes through the other door, the one that leads into the service area, wipes her sticky hands on her apron. "What can I get you?" she asks the young man with the floppy hair.

He brushes aside a clump of it and she can tell straight away he's a junkie, and a junkie who hasn't had his fix recently. His eyes seem to sparkle, to vibrate, and one of them is delicately swollen.

"Coffee," he mumbles. "Black. Six sugars."

Katja pours him a cup from the grumbling machine behind her, takes her time as she turns back to survey the customers once more. They all look normal, genuine—but how could she be sure? What if one of them had . . . ?

Stop it.

She pushes the cup in front of the junkie and gives him a sugar bowl.

"Knock yourself out," she says.

And she's looking at the smiling trucker again because

9

he's looking at her.

She turns away, grabs a cloth and cleans the same spot on the counter over and over.

What now? What now?

What the fuck had she gone to the diner for anyway? To pretend everything was normal? To whom?

To whom?

Shit. Shit. Shit.

But she has the vial, she has her ticket off the island.

Not quite.

She tries to slow her thoughts down, tries to grab a hold of them so she can focus on them properly.

She has the vial, yes—but she doesn't have Januscz, and those waiting for the vial would be expecting them both. So what now?

There is laughter and she turns to the booth with the men playing cards. The trucker looks up at her once again but this time he isn't smiling.

He knows, she thinks, *he knows. How can he know?*

Stop it. Stop it. He doesn't know. If he did why wouldn't he just go straight to her and take the vial?

He doesn't know.

She needs to get out of there, Katja realizes. She went to the diner because she was already late for her shift and didn't want to arouse any more suspicion, because she had panicked, but now she realizes she has to get out of there. The trucker probably doesn't know what she's done but it will only be a matter of time until someone comes along who does.

Shit, they would know where she works, they would know where to come.

Get out. Take the vial and get the fuck out of here.

But she isn't going to get anywhere without Januscz, and she doesn't think it likely he will be turning up any time soon to help her.

Not considering the state she had left him in.

He goes up to the junkie and she says to him, "I need your help."

He doesn't seem to register the request at first, then looks up. His eyes fix on her lip ring, sparkling in the harsh lighting. He seems transfixed by it.

"Huh?"

"Do you have a car?"

"Huh?"

"Do you have a car?"

His fingernails are adorned with chipped nail polish and he wears thick leather straps around each wrist. "A car?"

"Yes. Do you have a car?"

He nods.

"Then I need your help. I need you to drive me somewhere," Katja tells him.

"Drive?"

He looks like he's still catching up on her first question, still processing it.

He chews on one of his fingernails.

"I need to get to the docks. I'm meeting someone there. Will you drive me?"

"Uhhh. The docks?"

"Yes. I'm meeting somewhere there. Can you take me?"

He looks around at the others in the diner and begins to say something but his tongue becomes wrapped around whatever substance he's still riding and it's nonsense that comes out. He takes a sip of his coffee and winces at its heat and/or sweetness. Chews his nail.

"I think some people might be after me," Katja adds to see if it will spur him on. "I think I might be in danger."

"Uhhh . . . yeah. Uhhh. Yeah."

He takes another sip of his coffee, looks around once more.

"Hey," Katja snaps. "Are you listening to me?"

"Mmmm," the man says. "Yeah . . . you want me to drive you."

"Yes."

"To the docks."

"Yes."

And she's beginning to think perhaps she should have asked someone else.

Anyone else.

"Okay," he says. This fucked-up druggie says. "Sure."

"Good. Can you take me now? I need to get there now."

"Uhhh, sure. Uhhh, yeah."

Katja looks across at the truckers and now they're all staring back at her. The one that smiled at her before, he isn't smiling any more. She sees his jaw muscles working.

"I'm going to go out the back way. Wait a minute then go out the front. There's an alley that leads up the side of the building. Meet me there. Okay?" The man nods and Katja goes back through into the kitchen. She reaches into the drawer and for some reason panics that the vial won't be there anymore but it is, it is there. She picks it up and puts it back in her pocket. Takes off her apron and stuffs the garment into the pot of chili. She's about to walk out when she hears the junkie shout, "Hey."

Her heart rate raises again and she pokes her head through the service window. The junkie is leaning over the counter slightly, conspiratorially.

"What?" Katja asks.

And he whispers loudly, "How much is it for the coffee?"

CHAPTER TWO

She's watching beads of sweat like glass balls tumbling from his brow and he's leaving smears of wet handprints on the steering wheel as he constantly adjusts his grip. The car is a battered old thing and looks about as secure as the man who is driving it but she has no other choice. She doesn't even know what a clutch does.

It's still raining outside and it's starting to get dark too. In one hand she's holding the vial she took out of her pocket when she climbed into the car in case it cracked or split. Even if she had anywhere else to put it, she is too preoccupied to bother hiding it from the man. She notices him glance at it then look away several times.

Finally she says, "This is what I've to take to the docks."

She uncurls her palm and lets the vial roll along her fingers. First joint. Second joint. Third. The liquid inside sparkles.

He seems too disinterested to not be interested.

And it only occurs to her now as she sits spinning it around and around in her palm that she could have made a mistake in picking a junkie to help her. He chews on a nail as he considers the vial.

But he doesn't ask what it is.

"I need to pick up some stuff first," she says. "I need to get my stuff."

She gives him directions to her squat and looks over her shoulder, watches the headlights behind them to see if they are being followed. The rain batters against the hood of the car, a hundred little explosions of light and water and she finds herself thinking of a similar wet burst that had come from Januscz.

And then, in the silence, the junkie says, "You're from that punk band aren't you? The Stumps. You played at King Tut's last week?"

Katja doesn't say anything, feeling a little exposed.

"I remember you because of your . . ."

His eyes trail across the plastic tube sticking out of her throat. His words drift.

"You were good," he says instead.

"It's a tracheostomy tube," she tells him, ignoring the compliment. "My name's Katja."

And she thinks shit, should have made a name up, but it's too late now and does it really matter anyway?

"Nikolai," he says.

"Nice to meet you, Nikolai."

He swings the car around a bend, past the garish neon glow of porn signage and in the paranormal lighting women stalk with gazelle legs and heavy coats wrapped around themselves. They are only a few blocks away from the squat now and she finds herself hoping it's either very busy or very quiet there.

"I have something to confess, Nikolai," Katja says. "I need you to help me out a little more than just driving me to the docks."

Nikolai doesn't take his eyes from the road ahead and she isn't even sure if he registered what she said. "Huh."

Should she tell him? She has to tell him. There is no point in her risking involving him as she already has if she isn't going to go all the way through with it.

"This vial, there's a man waiting for it on a boat going to the mainland tonight."

"The mainland?"

The mainland. Which meant that whatever was happening definitely wasn't legal.

"You want to get off this fucking shit-tip island, Nikolai?"

"I . . ."

"'Course you do. Everybody does. That's why they work so hard to keep us all here. That's why the only boats that come to and from the island are either bringing shit or taking it. But I can get you off the island, Nikolai. Tonight. Do you have any friends or family?"

"I . . . no . . ."

"Good. Then you've got no reason to stay here?"

"I guess not," he says slowly and finally looks at her.

"Next left," Katja says. "My boyfriend, my ex-boyfriend, shit he wasn't even really a boyfriend, just someone I hung out with and fucked every once in a while, but that's not important. Anyway, he works for this guy, this guy named Dracyev and he's a dealer, right, he's a chemical dealer and he asked Januscz, that's my boyfriend, he asked Januscz to make this exchange tonight, on the boat, to give this guy, this other guy, not Dracyev, to give him this vial."

"The vial," Nikolai says.

"Yeah, the vial. I don't know what the fuck is in it, who the hell knows with those guys. I never liked Januscz being involved in that shit, but then again he never liked me screaming my head off every other night and coming home with blood crusting my trach tube, but that's not important right now, okay?"

Nikolai chews his nail, works on it. He stops at a set of lights and waits patiently.

"Anyway, Januscz is meant to meet this guy tonight but the problem is, see, the problem is he can't really do that anymore because we kind of got into an argument because the fucker, the fucker he was going to take this shit and split to the mainland and he never said a fucking word to me, he never said one goddamn word to me, he was just going to do this deal and get his ass over to the mainland and he was meant to take me you know, he was meant to. Dracyev had arranged it so we could both go, but Januscz was going to go without me."

"Was?"

17

"Yeah, was, 'cause I found out what he was planning and I kind of lost it a little, I guess, and I sort of shot him."

"Shot him?"

"Just in the neck or the shoulder or somewhere around there, I'm not sure because I didn't stick around long enough to make sure, you know—plus, what the hell difference does it make anyway?"

"Is this the place?" Nikolai asks, pulling onto a quiet street lined with old buildings scarred with graffiti and broken windows. There are several vehicles parked ahead of them but only one that looks drivable.

"Just at the end here," Katja tells him. "I need to get some stuff first, you know? At the end there. Anyway, so I sort of shot Januscz and then I just took off because I thought if someone finds out what I've done, well, you know, some serious shit is going to happen so I figure well, fuck, he was going to screw me over and leave without me anyway so I'll do the same to him. Here. Just here."

And Nikolai pulls the car over to the curb next to a building in a worse state than most. The steps leading up to the main doorway are partially blocked by two dumpsters stacked end-on-end, and there is the faint sound of bass-heavy music coming from inside.

"But this guy who's going to make the exchange, well, he's expecting Januscz and me to turn up, right, the both of us together, so he's going to figure something's up if it's only me and I'm not the mule, right, I'm not Dracyev's man, so I need you, I need you to act like you're Januscz, pretend to be Januscz, that is."

"But won't he know I'm not . . . ?"

"Januscz isn't a player, not the player he thinks he is. He's never done anything like this before, a deal I mean. I don't know why the fuck Dracyev has suddenly decided he can trust a loser like Januscz to do this sort of thing but he has, he did, so this guy that's waiting for him, for me, for us, on the boat, he's wearing a red suit. This guy has never seen or met Januscz before. He's just been told to wait for a guy and a girl with this vial coming tonight, and in exchange to help them get to the mainland. A red suit."

"Right."

"So I need you to be Januscz. Pretend to be, I mean. Will you do that?"

"Just say I'm Januscz?" Nikolai asks.

"Just say you're Januscz. Then we'll be taken to the mainland and we can leave the vial with this guy or take it to someone on the other side or whatever the fuck was meant to happen and then we're out of there and you can do whatever you want once you're there. I just need your help to make this exchange."

"And I can get off the island? With you?"

"Yes. I just need to get my stuff first."

Nikolai nods and for the first time seems lucid, fully comprehending. "From here?"

"From here. Just wait for five minutes. Keep the engine running."

"Okay."

And she smiles, or grimaces at least, and gets out of the car. She is aware of a small handful of people lingering in doorways and the alleys that run between the buildings, but she knows the area well and knows that there are always people lingering in the darkness and shadows. Regardless, she keeps them in her field of vision as she presses herself through the gap between the two dumpsters and climbs the steps.

The front entrance has long been nailed shut so she walks around to a stack of packing crates leaning up against one of the walls. In the rain she slides the crates to one side and reveals a gap in the brickwork that probably started as a small hole but has since been worked into an opening big enough for her to crawl through.

The others in the squat have their own entrances, through corroded iron plates bolted over the lower floor's windows to ramps that lead up to damaged roofing, each inhabitant like a separate species of insect, creating their own personal nests.

She drops down into the basement chamber that passes for her own nest and instantly feels a strange mix of security and vulnerability. Of claustrophobia.

Home.

Punk posters litter the walls, curling where the tape that holds them up has weakened and come away. Packets and wrappers lie like shed skins and there are audio cassettes scattered across the floor. Several guitars sit propped up against a large, stained amp in one corner.

She grabs one of the guitars, a battered black one with stickers scarring it like surgical wounds. The logos of other local bands and some from the mainland. The torn fragments of dead idols. The renowned and honourable mission statement of the Zapatistas—everything for everyone . . . and nothing for ourselves.

She slips the guitar over her neck backward so it hangs at an angle down her spine, then tightens the strap to hold it more firmly to her body. She turns to decide what else she needs to take, just the important stuff, just whatever she can't live without, when she hears the voice.

"Katja."

The man is standing in the doorway to her room, wearing a jet black suit with a rounded collar like that of a priest, and has a thick gold earring in one ear. He carries a clipboard loaded with paper in one hand and a dictation machine in the other.

The man is Anatoli Aleksakhina and he is her parole officer.

"What the fuck are you doing here?" she asks him. She has the vial in her hand, not wanting to risk leaving it in the car with the junkie, and now regrets it. "How did you get in?"

"You were meant to come to the station today to check in."

"I forgot," she says. "I've been busy."

"Katja, you should know by now that isn't acceptable."

"I know, I know, I'm sorry. I . . . there was a car accident and I . . ."

"You're going to need to come to the station with me."

Katja's heart trip hammers. Her guitar is now strapped too tightly to her to allow her to swing it around like she often did at her gigs, to allow her to turn it into a weapon—again, as she often did at her gigs. Instead she considers the big heavy bass guitar that lies against the wall between herself and Aleksakhina.

"I can't," she tells him. "I'm late for my shift at the diner. I was just stopping off for a change of clothes. I got soaked when I went to help at the car accident."

"The car accident," Aleksakhina repeats. "And where was this?"

"Across town," she answers immediately.

"Has it been reported? Because I could call now and . . ."

"No. I mean . . . yes. I mean, I saw someone else calling. Someone else called. Anyway, there's no working phones here. Not anymore. But someone's called already. I think I heard sirens."

"You're still going to need to come with me."

And Katja is moving, slightly, just slightly, toward the bass guitar. It feels like she's been in the room for hours and hopes the junkie will still be waiting for her outside.

"I can't," she insists. "My shift."

"You're taking your guitar to the diner?"

"I have a gig later. But I need to get to work."

"I'll call your manager. Explain."

"I could come later, after I'm finished. I was going to do that anyway."

"And what time do you finish?"

"A little after two AM, usually."

"Well that's no good, is it? The conditions of your parole were that you should check in with me once a week. The last time I spoke to you was last Thursday. If you call me after your shift then that will be eight days, not seven."

Katja's jaw flexes. She clamps down on her anger. "Come on. Give me a break."

"I've already given you several breaks, Katja. That's why you're on parole and not on month two of an eight-month stretch."

"It's two hours," she says, moving closer again to the bass. "What the fuck difference does it make? Please, I've got to get to my shift. It's rehabilitation, right?"

Aleksakhina shakes his head. "Sorry, Katja. You're going to have to come with me."

"No."

And her hand squeezes the vial reflexively.

"What have you got there?" Aleksakhina asks.

Katja snatches her hand behind her back then brings it out again slowly when she realizes it's too late. "Nothing," she says weakly. Then, "Medicine. For my throat."

Aleksakhina doesn't buy it. "What are you involved in now, Katja?" he asks, and his voice is like that of a father who has discovered his daughter's dope stash.

"I'm not involved in anything. I just want to get to my work."

"Not tonight. Tonight you're coming with me."

Her face flexes involuntarily, an open display of distaste, and Aleksakhina reads it well because he takes another few steps and is now closer to the bass guitar than Katja. He extends his open hand to her.

"I can't," she tells him.

"Give it to me, Katja. We can discuss this back at the station."

"I can't go to the station. Not tonight. I promise, I'll be there first thing in the morning."

"You said a minute ago you'd come after your shift was done." He is now holding a pair of handcuffs.

"Fine, whatever."

"Give me the vial."

Her nostrils flare and she slowly, reluctantly, hands it to him. She tongues her lip ring nervously as he looks it over but either he doesn't recognize the significance of the watermark on the glass or he doesn't care because he just puts it in his pocket.

"Come on," he says, almost touching her arm. He pops one of the cuffs open. "With me."

Again Katja's nostrils flare and again she finds herself considering the bass guitar but now he has the vial, so she can't risk attacking him and breaking it. *Fuck. Fuck. Fuck. Fuck. Fuck.*

"Okay," she says finally and lets her head flop dramatically to her shoulders as her third liberty spike already has. "I'll come. But are those things really necessary?"

"With you? Yes," he says as he snaps the cuffs on her.

They go back out through the room's main door, not the hatch Katja crawled through. If there is anyone else in the squat at the time, then they are certainly making themselves scarce. If they in any way helped Aleksakhina find her then they were certainly better off doing so. Cuffs or not, Katja is ready to do some damage.

But the place is silent as she is led up the untrustworthy staircase toward the front door. The parole officer knows not to bother trying to open the door itself, instead pushes aside a flap of corrugated iron that conceals another opening. He gestures for Katja to go through first.

And she thinks of the junkie as she bends down, having to angle herself to stop the butt of her guitar catching on the rim of the opening, using it as an excuse to go slowly. As she eases herself through, she notices Nikolai's car still parked farther up the street, partially obscured by the dumpsters, and the engine is still running as she instructed.

Aleksakhina is right behind her, pushing his way out into the rain.

She could run, she thinks, sprint over to the junkie's car and maybe throw herself in the back seat before Aleksakhina knows what is going on and then the two could be speeding off again. But to where? Aleksakhina has the vial, and there was no way she could grab it back from him while still cuffed—not without the risk of breaking it.

So what?

What now?

Nikolai will get a clear view of them once they start toward street level but she can't risk him doing anything that might mean the vial getting broken.

"Come on."

And Aleksakhina has a hand on the small of her back, and they go down the steps to the pavement, slip between the dumpsters. Katja glances back at Nikolai and he is still sitting there behind the wheel. The engine is running. The lights are off. Aleksakhina's car is on the other side of the road and he leads her toward it, opens the rear door and puts her inside. She has to lean forward slightly because of the guitar. As the man settles into the driver's seat, Katja looks over her shoulder and Nikolai is still in the car.

She doesn't know if she wants him to come across or not. Perhaps it will be easier to come up with another plan, to dump the junkie while she can and get someone more reliable to help her. One of her band mates.

Of course.

Her band mates.

"Are you arresting me?" she asks through the metal grating that separates her from the front of the vehicle. "Do I get a phone call?"

"We'll see," Aleksakhina tells her, and drives off. He turns the car around and they pass Nikolai.

And he's still sitting in the driver's seat.

Fucking useless junkie.

PART TWO
FUCKING USELESS JUNKIE

CHAPTER THREE

He's smiling, Nikolai.

He's smiling because he has the money in his hands now and it feels real, it feels as good as a thick, heavy baggie of really pure stuff or a nice big sparkling rock straight out of the labs of one of the chemists. He has it wrapped up safely inside a plastic bag stuffed inside his coat and his arms are folded across his chest to protect it.

He worries that someone might come and snatch it from him because he's done it himself in the past and here, in the area he's at now with the streets acne'd with porn shops and liquor stores, he is at even greater risk than elsewhere. So he keeps himself to himself as he shuffles toward Kohl's games arcade and ignores the enticements of the street girls who stumble after him and the dealers whose wares he doesn't trust. He lets his hair fall before his eyes and focuses on the reflection of the arcade's glittering lights, letting them draw him in.

The horrible, clawing feeling that has been lurking in his veins for the past few days has faded as this moment has grown closer. The release will not be far off. The voodoo splatter of sound effects blasts over him as he steps over the entrance to the arcade and a smile splits his face. Games cabinets stretch out on either side of him and the place is alive with all kinds of energy, drunk with it. He recognizes a few other players and they nod to him as he passes but he pays them no attention—there will be time for that later.

He heads straight for the booth that sits cage-like in the middle of the place. It is hexagonal, plated variously with reinforced glass, thick plastic, and scratched pieces of metal. Trapped inside it, its prisoner, is a morbidly obese woman who looks as if she is in there for life, held fast by the thick wedges of adipose tissue that seem to be inflated around her. Her hair is grey-blonde and wiry. Her arms are full of blue veins and he can see them pumping blood around. He becomes mesmerized by their beat and she has to snap him out of it by slamming her fist against the glass before him.

"The fuck you back here for?" she asks. She wears a headset that bites into the soft flesh of her cheek. Her voice comes through a speaker mounted on the side of the hexagon, static-sharp.

Nikolai tears his eyes from those pulsing veins of hers, then has difficulty deciding whether to speak to her face or to the dislocated voice coming from the speaker. He ends up going back and forth between the two like a puppy that can't decide which treat to take.

"I need to see Kohl," he tells her.

She blows a bubble from the bright pink gum she is chewing on, pops it. "Uh huh."

Blows another bubble. Pops it. Her tongue is fat and veiny.

Nikolai grins uncontrollably, screws his feet against the ground. Taps the speaker.

"Hello?" he says into it. "I need to speak to . . ."

"I heard you. He's busy."

There is the mechanical stutter of gunfire coming from one of the game machines. The whine of a bomb dropping in another. This is a warzone, a private little warzone.

Nikolai bites down on a finger nail, tastes the bitterness of a piece of polish flaking off in his mouth. "Can I . . . ? Do you . . . ? I need to speak to him."

"You as dumb as you look?" the woman blurts. She raises her head and Nikolai is pushed aside by another joystick junkie who shoves notes at her through a gap in the window. The woman pumps a lever and coins spill out across the counter. The man collects them all in a plastic bag then hurries off.

Nikolai is clenching and unclenching his fists. His mouth moves but he cannot summon the words.

Then, "Please. Tell him it's Nikolai. Tell him I need to see him."

"Oh, *Nikolai*," the fat woman says. "Well why didn't you say so in the first place?"

Nikolai sighs, relaxes. Nods. "Yeah, Nikolai."

And the woman's expression changes instantly. "He's busy, Nikolai. Now fuck off, I have customers waiting."

Nikolai looked behind him. "There's nobody . . ."

"Fuck. Off."

"I have money."

"That'll be a first."

And he reaches into his coat and takes out the plastic bag just far enough that she can see the thick wad of notes inside. He leaves it there hopefully, tilting it from side to side as if that will somehow entice her further.

Finally the woman pops a final bubble. "Let me see if he's around," she says.

Nikolai grins and lets the woman chatter into her headset for a few moments.

"He says he'll send someone down for you in a minute. Go wait for him out back."

Nikolai shoves the baggy back into his coat, locks his arms around it once more, and shuffles off. He is quickly consumed by the Atari blitz, the stench of sugary drinks, and the metallic odour of the hot machinery. He rolls across to the back door, shadowed and hidden by the glow of the games, and leans against the nearest cabinet.

A young girl is playing, two fists wrapped around the little joysticks, snapping them back and forth in unison, her face still and expressionless. Flickers of hope or frustration every now and again. She is lost in the electronica and he knows the feeling well.

The world is shed. It crumbles and falls away like

damaged brickwork. It is fake and surreal and once it is all gone there is only a pure blackness and you are floating in amongst it. Nothing touches you.

You are safe.

A hand snaps onto Nikolai's shoulder, the fingers long and thin, seeming to have more joints than they should.

And it is a woman and she bulges with steroid musculature. She is wearing loose gym trousers and a triangular bikini top, her body like polished amber glass. She looks Nikolai up and down as if he is something that has just been coughed up by a pneumonia-ridden old man.

"Nikolai," she says, half question, half statement.

He feels her hand sinking into the soft flesh of his shoulder as if she is seeking out the weakened tissue beneath, trying to determine his body fat ratio by touch alone. She sneers almost imperceptibly and turns.

"Come with me."

And they go through the door and up a set of steps that shine as eagerly as her follicle-free skin, and Nikolai watches her muscles moving like little creatures trapped inside her. His tongue feels swollen. It is eager for the sparkling grains that Kohl will bring it in the next few minutes.

The muscled woman leads him to a door at the end of the corridor, though he already knows where to go since he has been there many times before. She crosses her thick arms and stands to one side.

Nikolai grins nervously as he slips past her and into the room beyond. The door closes.

The place is like a graveyard for games machines

KATJA FROM THE PUNK BAND

with gutted cabinets lining each wall and their cracked
and burnt innards spilling out of them. There are several
windows but they are all blacked out with a thick, dark
plastic. In the middle of the room is a large workbench,
and the man leaning against the workbench looks like a
human-bug hybrid because of the globular wraparound
goggles he wears.

They have a dark red tint that reflects the errant flashes
of light coming from the games still struggling to survive.

This is Kohl.

"Nikolai." Again—half question, half statement.

Nikolai remains by the door, taking comfort in the exit
it offers him, trying not to think about the woman that still
guards it on the other side.

"I need some . . . new . . . stuff," he says to Kohl.

Kohl is holding a circuit board in one hand. Next to
him a handheld blowtorch kisses the air with a blue-white
flame. "Your type always do."

Nikolai puts a nail between his teeth. "I have money."

He offers the bag to Kohl, who considers it for a few
moments. Then he holds out his hand and Nikolai lets him
touch it but won't let it go. Kohl snatches it from him, tears
away the plastic and counts the notes.

"Where does someone like you get this sort of money?"

Nikolai licks his lips. His tongue is fat and cumbersome
in his mouth. His spine itches with chemical need.

Where indeed.

DJ Nazarian hasn't left this place for close-on six months

so it is entirely fitting that he should die here.

This place is a space like the engine room on a large tugboat except that it is perched atop a high rise in the middle of the city and, while it still worked, operated the lifts that ferried those who used to live there up and down the thirty-nine floors. That machinery is now cold and dead, just like Nazarian, but the machinery that he brought with him, that which allowed him to ride the airwaves for so long, is sparkling and new.

Apart from squats in the few apartments that were still livable, the high rise is long-deserted. It has been marked for demolition and had all the windows and floorboards removed in preparation but it seems as if the day will never come that it will be put out of its misery.

When Nikolai first walks in he notices some of the equipment is still set to broadcast mode, and he wonders if it is even now feeding the sound of his tentative footsteps, of his voice calling for the pirate DJ, out across the city. Nazarian is sprawled on the floor, blood-stained vomit having erupted from his mouth and down his neck. He is still holding the baggy of whatever it was he took, though there is nothing but a few particles left over.

Nikolai bends down beside him and this isn't something new to him, finding one of his friends dead on the floor next to the cause of their death—be it powder, pill, or blade. He knows that one day he will end up the same. He is kneeling next to himself.

He looks around at the shelves full of hi-fi equipment, the cables that snake across the ground like the lights of automobiles in a time-delayed photograph, the miniature satellites that aim toward the glassless windows, toward the city outside. Nazarian had been a friend, a welcome voice filtered through static and bad air. He surely wouldn't have wanted all the equipment to go to waste.

And there would be other pirates willing to make use of it, of course.

Nikolai decides he would be doing the pirate DJ a favour.

"A friend," Nikolai tells Kohl, looking down at the money.

"You must have some good friends," Kohl says. "This'll do nicely."

And a smile breaks on Nikolai's face.

He watches Kohl take the money and stuff it in his back pocket.

The two stare at each other for a few moments, Kohl stock still, Nikolai twitching nervously.

"Ermmm . . . ?"

"Was there something else?" Kohl.

"I . . . what about . . . ?"

"What? Speak up. Can't hear you."

"The stuff," Nikolai say. The hairs are standing up on the back of his neck, his palms sweating. Each tiny beep echoing from the speakers of the games cabinets pierces him like a bullet.

"What stuff would that be? Look, I'm busy here. Could you see yourself out?"

Nikolai almost started toward the door automatically then caught himself. "I . . . don't understand. I gave you the money . . ."

Like everyone, he's had deals go bad on him before and that was why he had given the money away reluctantly, as if it were some sort of afterthought or minor gesture. But Kohl isn't some street punk, some piece of shit selling fickle grams at a time. He is one of those you go to when you have enough money to mean you don't have to worry about being double-crossed.

But now this.

"And I've taken your money and it covers some of what you already owe me," Kohl tells him. "Thanks for the payment. Now get the fuck out."

The man goes back to the circuit board in his hands, tilts the blowtorch at it. The flame bursts forth bright and harsh and threatening.

"Kohl, please. I'll pay you what I owe you, I will. But I need something for now."

"You don't have any money for now."

Nikolai thinks quickly, desperately. "I can get some more money. Please."

"It's taken you four weeks to come up with this, Nikolai, where the hell are you going to get even more money before the end of tonight? Rob another one of your junkie friends?"

"I can get the money," Nikolai lies. If he can just get enough to see him through the next few days, he'll be able to figure out what to do next, but there's no way he can come up with a decent plan while still so spun.

"You're not getting a thing until I get the rest of what you already owe me." Kohl flames the circuit board. The smell of hot metal pirouettes into the air, pure energy.

"*Kohl.*"

And Nikolai has a hold of Kohl's arm and immediately knows he's done the wrong thing, but before he can take it back the other man swings around, drops the circuit board and the hand now wraps around Nikolai's skinny throat, squeezes. Kohl lifts him clean off the ground and drives him across the room and into a wall, pins him there.

The blowtorch wavers before Nikolai's face. Kohl's eyes are swollen by the curving plastic of his glasses, and the story goes that he almost burned them out while high on one of his varied concoctions playing Space Invaders for seventeen straight hours and now needs the bubble-like protection to stop him going completely blind.

That's the story.

Or one of them.

A whine escapes Nikolai's nose and he's too afraid to say anything.

The blowtorch flame roars across his neck.

"If you ever want me to even *consider* selling you or any of your junkie friends anything ever again then you'll do what's good for you and get the fuck out of my joint right now."

He says it softly, soothingly, and it confuses Nikolai's soggy comprehension further, takes him a few moments to recognize the threat. Another wave of the blowtorch confirms this.

"Misha!" Kohl shouts through the door and the muscled woman barges her way in just as Kohl shoves Nikolai toward her. Without a moment's hesitation she lashes out and hooks Nikolai heavily and cleanly across the chin, dropping him to the ground like he'd been shot in the head.

Little blossoms of light fill his vision and they bloom into great bright explosions as he is lifted onto his feet once more and then there is a second, greater impact in his stomach that doubles him up. The only thing that stops him collapsing to the ground once more is the fact that the woman has a hold of his hair.

His head is pulled upward abruptly and his neck makes an uncomfortable snapping sound. He squints through the pain and sees Kohl's bug-eyes looming before him.

"You bring me the rest of what you owe me by tomorrow night, Nikolai. Then we can talk further."

Nikolai starts to speak, feels the metallic taste of blood roll across his tongue and dribble down his chin. "I . . ."

And that's all he can manage before he is being dragged down the stairs then through the electron massacre of the arcade before being dumped onto the wet street.

He lies there for some time, vaguely aware of those that are passing him, of the deals being done and bodies bought and sold. Finally he opens his eyes and the ground beside him is awash in garish, reflected neon. His mind catches up with what has just happened and he sits up.

"Fuck."

CHAPTER FOUR

So Nikolai is fucked, good and proper, robbed of the one piece of good luck that he has had lately, robbed of the spoils of his dead friend's equipment and so he's doing what he always does when he doesn't have drugs to lose himself in and that is to lose himself in games instead.

He's already sold all of the cabinets that he once had and so all he has left is a stripped-down cocktail cabinet, the sort that you sit down and lean over to play. The protective glass that once topped the device is gone, as are the original legs, which have been replaced by concrete blocks stolen from a nearby building site. The hatch that allows access to the circuit board within is also gone and he can feel the heat from the machine emanating against his knees.

His left eye has swollen slightly from the impact of Mischa's punch and he takes comfort in the fact that the pain from his stomach is at its least powerful when he bends over as he does when he plays the game.

In the background, a TV is playing an old black-and-white Soviet propaganda cartoon from which he takes a strange comfort.

He's mumbling curses to himself as he jams the control buttons and joystick, dictating the elaborate revenges he will commit upon the dealer Kohl.

". . . shove that blowtorch up his . . ."

Slaps the two control buttons one after another.

". . . fucking motherfucking blind motherfucker . . ."

Grits his teeth and just avoids dropping another credit as a pixilated laser beam shoots past the ill-shapen spacecraft he is controlling.

". . . show him how to . . ."

And there is a knock at his door.

He doesn't hear it at first but then it repeats and he stops playing.

A tiny explosion erupts below him as his spaceship is destroyed and the funeral march sounds, midi-style.

"Open up, Nikolai."

"Oh fuck."

Kohl.

Nikolai jumps back from the machine as if he has just received a shock from it and his neurons start firing randomly once again.

"Nikolai!"

And he's looking around for an exit; the window that opens out onto the stairs that are stapled to the side of the building and lead down to the dumpsters below, the aged garbage chute that has been blocked since before Nikolai moved in a year before and whatever it is that blocks it, it stinks.

He's going round and round in circles, a dog chasing its tail.

And then the door bursts open and he stumbles backward, into the games machine and over it, tumbling to the floor with an almighty thud. He tries scrambling to his feet but Kohl has grabbed him already and Nikolai raises his hands to his face defensively.

"Don't! Don't!"

He is pulled upright into a sitting position, his back against the apartment's rear wall.

"Shut up, shut up," Kohl snaps.

And Nikolai struggles but Kohl has a firm grip of him and he can go nowhere, do nothing.

"What the fuck?! It's only been a few hours! I don't have . . ."

And Kohl slaps him, lightly, just to quieten him. Nikolai bites down on the rest of the sentence and it becomes a senseless gargle.

"Listen."

In the background is the sound of the cartoon, the comically exaggerated noises of a fight between a cat and some other indistinguishable creature. Perhaps an American.

"This place is a shithole," Kohl says as he looks around. He lets go of Nikolai and stands, walks amongst the trash that litters the room. "Haven't you ever heard of drawers?

Clothes hangers? For fuck's sake."

And Nikolai watches, still reeling from the dealer's sudden entrance, as Kohl starts picking up random pieces of clothing that have been left lying about.

"Where are these meant to go?"

And Nikolai doesn't understand at first, holds his cheek where it still stings from the man's slap. "I . . ."

"A closet? A rail? Anything?"

"I . . . in the bedroom."

And he watches as Kohl takes the pile he has collected and disappears into the bedroom. A moment passes.

"Jesus Christ!" Shouted through the open doorway. "This is disgusting!"

And Nikolai is still too confused to feel ashamed and he thinks that this must be what it is like to have a mother when you are growing up. "I'm . . . sorry . . . ?" he mumbles weakly.

He gets to his feet and tentatively looks into the bedroom. Kohl is shoving hangers from the bare wardrobe into the grotty, stained clothing he has picked up. He's wearing a pair of black rubber gloves that he's produced from somewhere.

"You know you get bugs growing in these things if you leave them lying around like this? They lay their eggs in your sweat and they hatch and it's a fucking infestation. Did you know that?"

"I . . . but . . ."

"No, of course you didn't. People don't care what's growing on them or in them. Order, Nikolai, it's important to have order, you understand?"

"Uh huh."

And Nikolai glances at the still-open front door, pictures the stairwell beyond and then . . . then what?

"Nikolai?! Are you listening to me?"

"Yes. I . . . Yes. What?"

"You see?" And Kohl steps to one side, presents the half-filled wardrobe. "That's all it takes, just a little bit of time and everything is in its place. You see?"

"Okay. I mean, yes. I see."

"Good. I certainly hope so."

And Kohl wipes his gloved hands on his trousers, grimacing as he does so.

"Now. As to why I'm here."

"I don't have it!" Nikolai yelps and he's leaning back through the bedroom door again. "You said tomorrow night!"

And then he stops and he thinks.

Shit. Is it tomorrow night?

How long has he been playing for?

"What day is it?"

But Kohl is shaking his head and smiling like a child who has been caught stealing. "I'm not here for the money, Nikolai. Not exactly."

Nikolai shoves a finger into his mouth, chews the top of the nail clean off. "So . . . ?"

"So I'm here to make a proposition. To provide you with an alternative."

"Uh."

The TV crackles into static as the cartoon ends.

"There's something I need, something I need you to bring me. Something I want."

"Okay."

"And if you can bring me it, then I'll perhaps be willing to disregard what you still owe me. And as an added thank you, give you this."

He holds up a small baggy of powder that sparkles white one moment and then the next moment a purple the colour of a fresh bruise, of a clean twilight.

A little line of perspiration raises on Nikolai's darkly stubbled upper lip. His body almost physically lurches at the sight of the drug and he has to stop himself from just grabbing it out of Kohl's hand, consequences be damned.

He knows Kohl will see the desperation in his eyes and he doesn't care.

"I can do that," Nikolai says as calmly as he can manage.

"Good, I'm glad. There is a man and he has this . . . object which I would like. I need you to go to him and take it from him. Then bring it back to me. Simple enough, even for someone like you."

The insult doesn't register but the implications of what Kohl might be asking of Nikolai do, and for the first time he feels hesitant.

"He'll be expecting me?"

"Not exactly, no. You might need to convince him to give it to you. You have a weapon?"

"You mean like a gun or something?"

"Yes, like a gun or something," Kohl says and his smile

falters momentarily.

"I have one somewhere, I guess."

"You guess?" Kohl snaps. He reaches into his pocket and pulls out a small pistol that is scratched and buffed on one side. He gives it to Nikolai barrel first, dropping the baggy into the man's hand at the same time.

Feeling safer now that he has the drug in his hand, Nikolai says, "I don't want to get involved in anything heavy, you know?"

Kohl's face hardens. "You mistake me for someone who cares."

Nikolai is suddenly aware that the gun is pointed at him, still partially in Kohl's hand.

"The man in question," Kohl says, "will be taking this object to mainland later tonight."

"The mainland?"

"But he won't get that far with it, right?"

The bulging red goggles loom in Nikolai's face.

"Right," Nikolai says weakly.

"Good. His name is Januscz. And this is his address."

CHAPTER FIVE

The place is in a nice part of town, but on the island there's an upper limit as to how nice places get and that limit is just below *slum*. It's nice in the sense that the windows are still in place and the fencing is intact. It's nice in the sense that Nikolai has walked along the street and not had to duck out of the way of roaming groups of youths who wouldn't think twice before engaging in a little game of junkie ball. Nice. But not really.

He's found a low wall around the back and has jumped into the overgrown garden and has been waiting in the bushes there, trying to figure out what to do next. The gun is in his pocket and his senses are sparkling from a hit of the drug Kohl gave him. It's something new, something different, and his body is taking time adjusting to it.

There's a dried-out swimming pool in front of him, the

cracked walls of which have been covered in tag art that bends and twists, and he has to pull himself away because he feels as if he is starting to be drawn in toward it. He jogs around it, toward the rear wall of the house. There are a set of large patio windows beyond another overgrown bush and he can see light and movement coming from within. And shouting.

He leans through the foliage of the bush, trying not to make any noise, looks in through the window. He sees a small kitchen constructed mostly from chrome that has lost all its shine and now resembles what he imagines the inside of his gun barrel to be like.

He watches for a few moments then catches a glimpse of someone striding past the door into the kitchen on the far side of the room and then a moment later another figure following quickly after. He is left with the impression of large spikes protruding from the figure's head but that can't be right.

The shouting continues but softens as the two go deeper into the house and Nikolai considers whether to stay at the window and hope they come back into sight, or try to follow the voices.

This is the man. This is the address.

Kohl had never mentioned anything about anyone else being there.

Shit. What now? What now?

Nikolai's gun hand flexes. He jogs around the side of the house and comes to another lower building stuck to the side—a garage. The wall is scabbed in the same graffiti as the swimming pool and makes his head dance as he slowly makes his way around.

Voices again. Shouting.

Something crashes around inside the garage and he's at once glad there are no windows and annoyed there aren't. Instead he listens and the shouting gets louder, another crash.

Then silence.

One beat.

Two beats.

Three beats.

And then the sound of a gunshot.

He jumps away from the wall and finds himself staring at the gun he holds as if to reassure himself that it wasn't his weapon that made the noise, that he hasn't fired it by mistake with his arcade-weary index finger.

He holds still, suddenly wanting to be away from there, regretting his desperation at agreeing to what Kohl had asked of him for the minimal hit he had needed. But it's done, it's done now and here he is at the stranger's house and a gun has been fired and now the door to the garage is opening noisily on the other side of the building.

He leans into the wall, holds the gun upright in his bent arm as he imagines you are meant to in situations like this.

And he hears a voice say, "Shit, shit, shit."

Then there is the sound of the door closing again, crashing down abruptly, and he hears movement back inside the house again. He rushes along the back wall, purely on instinct, and reaches the kitchen window just in time to see the spike-headed figure flash past going in the opposite direction from before, and so he continues along the rear wall until he reaches the other side and there he waits.

He presses a nail into his mouth and chews hurriedly on it.

Just enough time passes for him to consider leaving, abandoning the whole thing and just trying to find another way to get Kohl his money, when he hears a door open toward the front of the house. He waits a few moments, listening to the footsteps, then eases his way along the passageway created by the house's high wall and the overgrown bushes that line the next property. When he gets to the end he sees a girl with spiked hair lingering in the driveway that leads to the front door.

She stands amongst high, rain-dampened grass and pieces of long-abandoned building materials, turns back and forth from the house to the end of the driveway and the street beyond. She's got something in her hand and at first Nikolai thinks it might be a weapon, the gun responsible for the shot fired minutes before, then he sees it more clearly.

The girl turns again, again.

This is the object. *A vial. I need you to bring me this vial.*

And she holds up her hand, considers the object she holds, the glass tube.

And then she is gone, walking briskly down the driveway and out onto the quiet street outside and Nikolai swears to himself.

Kohl had said it would be easy. Just go to the house,

find the man, and get the vial. Go to the house, find the man, and get the vial.

Go to the house.

Check.

Find the man.

Check. The other figure he had glimpsed through the window must have been Januscz.

Get the vial.

Simple.

Simple.

Simple.

Get the vial.

So Nikolai jogs down the driveway after the girl.

He watches her until she disappears over the rise in the street then runs to his car and starts the motor. He drives as calmly and normally as he can manage, trying not to make it look as if he is following her, keeping his eyes straight ahead as he passes her. Pulls onto a side street farther up, waits again until she passes, drives on past her again and thankfully there is other traffic around in which he can hide.

He does this for almost ten minutes and it begins to rain and she quickens her pace and finally she dashes into a crappy-looking diner set back from the street and adjacent to a gas station. He parks outside, thinking she might have just been getting out of the rain but quickly grows nervous.

It doesn't feel safe or right to be sitting motionless in his car so he gets out, the gun still in his pocket, walks into the diner.

He looks around at the booths inside but doesn't see the girl and panics momentarily, thinking perhaps she had known she had been followed and already slipped out the bathroom window or some secret back entrance.

She might still be in the toilets.

Or she might already be half a mile away.

Gone. With the vial.

Shit.

He continues to the service counter and sits down because it seems like the thing to do. A waitress is wiping the surface before him.

Perhaps he'll go and check out the toilets.

And then he looks up and there she is, the woman, staring back at him through the little window on the other side of the service area, the great spikes of her hair beginning to droop under the weight of the rainwater.

"Be with you in a minute," she says to him.

He nods, panic washing over him and then leaving just as quickly.

She doesn't know.

She doesn't know.

Okay, so what now?

"What can I get you?"

And it's her and she's right in front of him, wearing an apron now. He brushes hair from his swollen eye as he looks up.

"Coffee," he mumbles. "Black. Six sugars."

And she pours him a cup and then hands him the sugar

bowl.

"Knock yourself out," she says distractedly, looking around the diner instead of at him. She begins to wipe the counter but isn't paying attention to that either. He thinks about using the payphone in the corner to call Kohl, ask him what to do next. Would he know who the girl was? And why she had shot the mule?

This was too much for him, too big. He wanted a simple deal, money for drugs, not this shit. Not this.

And what had she done with the vial?

He imagines himself taking out the gun, pressing it to her forehead and demanding the vial. And then he thinks about pulling the trigger but he stops himself, realizes it just feels too wrong.

And he thinks that he knows her from somewhere, somewhere completely out of context.

He looks at the phone again. Kohl.

Where was the vial?

What had she done with it?

Had she already slipped it to the other waitress? Was she just one part in a chain of transfers? Phone. The phone.

Kohl.

He chews his nails. Fuck.

He hasn't asked for any of this.

And he's just about to get up and phone Kohl when the girl, she comes up to him and she says, "I need your help."

CHAPTER SIX

So he's sitting in the car, engine running, in some part of the city that he's not familiar with, waiting for the girl, Katja, to come back out. His fingers rattle against the steering wheel and one more time he's certain that she's fucking him over somehow.

He is trusting that her story about getting off the island is for real and he's trying not to think about why she might have picked him to help her. He thinks about her when she was up on stage the previous week, glittering with sweat, not so much playing her guitar as physically abusing it, the little tube in her neck like a piece of strangely decadent jewellery.

He hears something farther down the street, looks in the rearview mirror and wonders if he is expecting to find Kohl standing there . He could still just take the vial from Katja, he wouldn't need to hurt her. He doesn't want to hurt her.

But then what? Take it to Kohl, get the money for another hit and a few days later he will be back to where he is now.

Then what?

He's never put as much thought as most into getting off the island because there was no reason to think that things would be any different on the mainland. It would just be another dealer, another type of drug. Another hit, another comedown. His life was cyclical anyway, what did it matter whether he couldn't get off the island?

But now, apparently, something matters. Something is giving him enough reason to want to break the pattern.

Katja.

What the fuck was she doing in that building anyway? he's just about to get out and go find out when he sees her coming out of the building, her guitar slung across her back like a Kalashnikov.

And there's someone with her.

Nikolai's heart rate begins to increase, he brushes his hair from his eye and touches the gun just to make sure it's there. Something is going on. This is it, this is the betrayal.

Kohl had set him up or she'd fed him the line about getting off the island just so he would bring her there and leave him outside waiting for her while she called on the man who would be his assassin, and now they were going to kill him and that would be that and . . .

They're walking away from him.

Toward another parked car farther up the street and it is black but patched with white blocks as if someone has vandalized it and the words have been painted over.

He notices Katja glance back at him surreptitiously. She's cuffed.

She's fucking cuffed.

Hands clenching on the wheel, on the gun. The engine still running.

Get out. Get out.

He's lost track of what was going on, become consumed by the night's events. Kohl and Katja and the vial and Januscz the courier. The dead courier. The gun, the guitar, the man in black that leads her to his car. Rain and soggy liberty spikes, punk music echoing in his head.

He finds himself unable to move as the man's car is started and Katja is still in the back, still cuffed. Were there others after the vial? Where were they taking her? Or was this just another part of some elaborate show designed to torment and punish him? His thoughts blossomed at the idea of some extensive plot involving the chemical gangs and their couriers and girlfriends and waitresses and just about everybody on the island, all knowing what was going on, playing with him, toying with him.

He ducks into his seat as the car sweeps past him and doesn't catch another glimpse of Katja though he tries to, wants to see the expression on her face, if she is still playing a part or whatever. And the car turns when it reaches the end of the road, is gone.

Shit.

Katja was gone, the vial was gone.

Kohl was still around, however. Waiting for the vial.

Waiting for Nikolai.

CHAPTER SEVEN

Back at his apartment, pacing from one end of the room to the other, listening to the sounds of the rolling demo from the games cabinet, trying to think of what to do next.

He had to get to the vial, had to get it. Had to help Katja. Or maybe it would be easier if he just took it and gave it to Kohl and fuck any thoughts about eloping with her to the mainland and those ideas he's been having about how maybe when they get to the other side they won't just go their separate ways but maybe she doesn't even have the vial any more, maybe she's dead, maybe she's fucking dead like Januscz, like stone-cold concrete, on the floor of some anonymous garage.

He presses his hands into his face, accidentally squeezes the bruising over his eye and yelps in pain, and there's a little bit of blood there. He goes to the bathroom and checks himself in the mirror, sees that he's split a welt that had formed at the top of his cheek. It looks like another eye, blinking at him as he wipes at it.

He opens a cabinet, searches for some iodine but instead his eyes settle on something else. It's a small cardboard box filled with old, crusted tubes. Vials.

Something he'd bought from a friend several months before, there had been a shot of some chemical in each one and though he normally never touched liquids, he'd been desperate at the time. He recalled how they tasted like stale lemons and how the only real affect they'd had on him was to irritate his bowels for a week.

He didn't even know where they came from.

He takes out one of the vials, rinses it under a quick blast of cold water and there's a watermark of some kind there, a little symbol that's only visible when the light hits it in a certain way.

This could work, he tells himself. How would Kohl even know?

He looks around for something to pour into the receptacle. Rejects old mouthwash because it's bright blue but then he hadn't gotten a good enough look at the stuff before to know what colour it was meant to be. Clear? Probably it would be clear. Or is that too obvious? doesn't know, doesn't know.

He glances at the toilet beside him.

A minute later and the vial is filled and he's shoving a stopper in it. He washes his hands to get the last of the urine off, holds the vial up to the light.

Should it be that colour? Surely that can't be healthy.

Stupid, stupid idea. There would be no way Kohl would fall for it, no way.

And now the phone is ringing.

The phone is ringing.

The fucking phone is ringing.

"Shit."

He turns off the tap, shoves the vial into his pocket, goes back through into the main room. He stares down at the phone as if he will be able to sense who is calling if he can just concentrate hard enough.

It could be Kohl.

It could be Katja.

Or it could be someone else entirely.

It's still ringing and he's chewing on a nail.

But Katja didn't have his number, how could she? Maybe she knew it already, maybe she really has been setting him up and she was going to warn him there was someone coming to get him, to finish him off for trying to steal the vial in the first place or maybe they thought he had Januscz or Katja had . . .

"Hello."

And he's picked up the phone just to make it stop ringing.

"You have the vial?"

Kohl. Fucking Kohl.

"Yes," Nikolai answers without thinking about it.

"Good. Wait for me there. I'm on my way."

And Nikolai begins to say something but the other man has already hung up. He drops the phone without putting it back on its cradle, strides to the front door, stops.

Has to get out of there.

Get away.

Fuck all this, fuck all of it, all he wanted was a single lousy hit, he never asked for any of this.

But what if they were waiting for him, ready for him to try and escape? He couldn't go out the front. Instead he turns and runs to the bedroom, slides open the window and climbs out onto the fire escape that leads down to the alley below. It's not the first time he's had to make a quick exit from the place and he's sure it won't be the last, if he is ever able to return.

He jumps over the balcony and jogs down the rattling steps two at a time, throws himself from the last set and lands awkwardly on the ground below. He grimaces in pain, turns over.

And is looking up at a set of gleaming red wraparound glasses.

Kohl takes a drag on the cigarette he holds.

"Going anywhere in particular?"

CHAPTER EIGHT

 was just . . ."

"Just . . . ?"

Nikolai can't think, can't speak.

"Where is it?" Kohl asks.

"I have it," Nikolai says.

"I know you have it, you just told me that." And Nikolai sees the phone in Kohl's hand. "So where is it?"

Nikolai licks his lips, sweeps his hair back. What else can he do?

He reaches into his pocket, gratefully finds the vial intact despite his hurried descent, and maybe it's just the street lighting but the colour looks even worse now as he hands it to Kohl.

The dealer examines it for a few moments and Nikolai almost decides to run there and then, just run and take his chances, but before he can Kohl says, "You did good, Nikolai."

"I did?"

Nods.

"There was a girl," Nikolai tells him. "I think it was a friend of Januscz's."

He doesn't know why he doesn't say girlfriend, though he isn't sure either way of their relationship. But he doesn't want to say girlfriend.

"A girl?"

"When I went to the house. There was a girl. I think they had an argument. A fight. She took the vial from him. Then I took it from her. I don't know what's going on with this shit but we're done, right? I did what you asked?"

Kohl is rolling the vial around between his fingers and Nikolai is certain he can smell his own piss.

Please, he begs. *Please*.

"You've done what I asked. And I'm grateful."

Kohl takes another, closer look at the vial. Nikolai tenses because now he is certain he can smell piss.

"You come round to the arcade later tonight and I'll have something special for you, okay?"

Nikolai nods. He feels as if he isn't there. He feels as if he's looking down on this conversation from his bedroom window.

And he just stands there numbly as Kohl walks away with the vial.

nd it's done now, he's done it, he's sold Kohl a fake.

Wriggled his way out.

He feels the deft lightness of relief as he climbs the rickety steps that lead back up to his apartment and grins at the added bonus of whatever it is Kohl will have waiting for him when he goes to the arcade later that night. As he gets near his apartment window, the air quality changes tangibly, thickens and acidifies. Clots.

He pulls himself in through the window and the motion seems to knock his momentary relief to the ground in one hard blast.

He'll find out. Kohl will find out.

Nikolai was lucky to have gotten the vial past him in the alley but surely he couldn't pass his own piss off as some new chemical drug forever? Kohl will know. He'll test it, find out it's a fake.

Or perhaps he already knows. Perhaps the story about Nikolai going back to the arcade later that night is a trick. They'll be waiting for him, the woman in the bikini and more, just waiting to punish him for thinking he could get away with this.

He ducks his head out of the window, suddenly certain there would already be a troupe of ogre-like bodyguards on their way up, impatient to get down to business.

Sees nothing.

He isn't safe.

He hasn't gotten away with anything.

All he's done is made things worse by not only fucking up on getting the vial but lying about it afterward. Nikolai has known people who have had their necks slit by dealers because they couldn't shit out the full contents of their stomachs and all the drug-stuffed condoms inside. He knows of a girl beaten to death because she tried to pay for her junk with her crumbling, angular body instead of hard cash. He knows of a man beheaded because he questioned the dealer's measuring of a shipment.

Nikolai, on the other hand, has faked an entire vial full of chemical and used his own bodily fluids to do so. How the fuck will Kohl take that when he finds out?

And Nikolai, he says aloud, "I'm fucking dead. Fucking dead!"

What the hell had he given Kohl the vial for? Why couldn't he have just told him the truth and said the girl had taken it, then was kidnapped? Kohl could surely not have held Nikolai responsible for that, or even if he had, at least it wouldn't have been as serious a betrayal as deliberately faking the vial.

"I should have just told him!" he shouts at the bare walls.

Bare except for a couple of bill posters stripped from the sides of boarded up buildings across town and one of them is for The Stumps.

Katja's band.

Kohl will find out what he has done, sooner or later. And when he does he will come looking for Nikolai and he will have plans—dirty, dark plans, plans that will most likely end with Nikolai stuffed into a container in an alleyway somewhere.

And he will find Nikolai because on the island there are only a small number of places where you can hide, and someone like Kohl, he will know every single one of them because he will probably have hidden in them himself at one point or another.

Therefore Nikolai knows that his only option is to get off of the island—and soon. Easier said than done.

There probably isn't a person on the island who isn't willing to do whatever it takes to get across to the mainland and the authorities know it, and they also know that they need to keep a handle on their captive workforce. To turn the handles and work the machines and drive the trucks and mould the plastics and bury the waste.

Getting off the island isn't something you do on a whim or without a seriously solid plan as to how you are going to do it.

But Nikolai, standing there looking at the poster, realizes he has one of those methods.

And she's out there, in the city, somewhere.

He knows he must find Katja and he also knows that means he will have to confront the man who kidnapped her.

PART THREE
THE MAN WHO KIDNAPPED HER

CHAPTER TEN

I have to go," he tells her.

"You can't go!" she shouts back, slamming her fists against the moist, dirty bed sheets.

He doesn't know how she gets them so dirty so quickly. He washes them every other day. Perhaps if she didn't spend so much time wrapped in them . . .

"But I have to," he says calmly, flinching at her anger. "I'll be as quick as I can, I promise."

"You always say that and I'm always left here! You're out all day; do you need to be out all night, as well?! What if something happens to me?!"

"Nothing will happen to you."

He is standing beside her, blocking the light from the streetlamp outside. His shadow is cast over her bony, pale face.

"How can you say that, Anatoli?!" she screeches. "Anything could happen! This headache...this headache..."

"You've already taken too many pills tonight. You'll give yourself a stomach ache."

"I already have a stomach ache," she says coldly. Accusingly.

"I'll be as quick as I can," he tells her, puts on his coat.

"You couldn't give a fuck about me! You care more about those criminal bastards than you do your own wife!"

He breathes, rolls with the comment just as he would roll with one of the punches or slaps she occasionally doled out. Accepts it numbly.

"If I don't work then I can't afford your medication," he says after a few moments as her fury hisses in the air, and then she is crying because he is about to leave and the shouting hasn't worked.

He sits on her bedside, takes her hand. She pulls herself up toward him, grips him more tightly than her supposedly weak frame should manage. He has to pry her from him and, as he shuts the bedroom door, he hears the TV flicker to life.

He stops by the phone on his way out and tries Katja's number one more time but, as before, there is no answer. So he steps out into the rain, stands before his car. The side of it is now patched up with white paint to cover the various vandalism attempts courtesy of the neighbourhood kids.

Now that they know what he does during the day.

It is probably only a matter of time before he will be

having to visit each of them, dragging them to and from courthouses and detention centres. He doesn't know whether it will bring him any satisfaction or not.

He starts the engine and drives across town to the aging brownstone that houses Katja's squat. He has been there before, knows which entrance she uses to get in. He lifts a piece of scrap metal lying on the overgrown lawn that runs up the side of the building and wedges it against some old rotten crates that he knows conceal a gap in the wall, just in case she tries to escape there. Then he walks around the back and squeezes himself through the pane of a long-vanished window that lies at ground level, drops into the room below.

The sounds of fucking hit him immediately and he turns to see a man and two women sprawled across a grubby mattress in the middle of the room. The man is sandwiched between the two women and Anatoli cannot make out whose limbs belong to whom. It is as if some mythical beast writhes before him until one of the women turns, crawls onto her knees toward him. She looks up at Anatoli, at his officious posture and the line of sweat rising on his brow and blade-like cheekbones.

She smiles invitingly, rolls her eyes as she is entered from behind by the other woman, wearing some sort of device strapped around her waist.

"Excuse me," Anatoli says, and leaves the room.

It is considerably cooler in the corridor. He wipes his brow with his sleeve and turns, notices a teenager with tattoos all down one side of his face at the same time that the teenager notices Anatoli, and the boy panics, drops the burger he is holding.

"Shit!"

And Anatoli tries to grab him, misses. "Wait!"

But some basic survival instinct has been triggered and the boy is gone, vanishing into the darkness farther down the hall, scurrying off into the innards of the building like a rat.

Anatoli walks to the third door on his left, leans into it.

Someone else is coming along the corridor now and their footsteps are slow, cautious. They too must sense his officialdom and that same survival instinct kicks in. Anatoli holds up a hand to stop them from running, let them know that whatever it is they've done, that's not why he's here.

He then enters the room and closes the door behind him.

"Katja?"

There is a bed, her guitars, an amp, some books. Little else.

She's not there.

It's possible she is in one of the other squatters' rooms but for people who spend their lives on hijacked property, Anatoli has found they are inordinately protective of their own little hiding holes. So she's not there and he doesn't really care that much.

It just doesn't seem that important.

But he'll give her ten minutes.

He crouches next to a stack amp, the mesh of which has

been ripped along one seam and is splattered with spray paint, feels the rumble of loud music filtering through the walls from one of the upper floors, and he's almost started drifting off to sleep when he hears movement nearby.

It's the rattle of the metal sheet he has placed up against Katja's entrance and there she is, her leg coming through now. He steps back into the deep frame of the room's doorway and it's enough to douse him in shadows and let him watch her for a few moments.

When she picks up her guitar he steps forward.

"Katja."

CHAPTER ELEVEN

She doesn't say a word when he piles her into the back of his car, just sits there as he drives. He's prepared for the fact that she might be lulling him into a false sense of security, ready to break free when he relaxes his guard, but just to be sure he tells her he just wants to talk to her.

She knows the drill though, knows that it's going to mean a night of detention if nothing else.

He drives through the rainstorm, and she knows the way to the station as if it is tattooed onto her soul, so when he pulls the car over to the side of a street several blocks away, she is instantly put on edge. Aleksakhina turns side-on so he can see her through the metal grate separating them.

Katja is itchy, nervous. She keeps looking around as if she expects something to happen, like a convict on death row awaiting the last-minute phone call that will call off the execution.

He can tell she wants to ask what's going on but she refuses to show any weakness or fear by asking and so decides to put her out of her misery.

"I could take you to the station right now, book you in. You'd most likely spend at least the night there but probably more."

Katja fingers the cuffs, squinting at the silhouette of the man, dissected by the metal between them. She finds other things to look at instead, thinking of how the upholstery is the same pale grey of a smoker's lung. He offers her a cigarette but she refuses.

"I could do that. But I want to give you a chance first."

"Let's just get this over with," she sighs.

"I thought we were finally getting somewhere, Katja," he says to her, flicking his lighter to spark his cigarette.

Her head is slumped to one side, her focus on a dark stain on the headrest.

Deliberately and obviously uninterested in anything he has to say.

"I don't want you to be here any more than you do. You think I've not got better things to be doing with my time?"

"Hey, don't let me hold you back," she says, still not looking at him. "If you've got a hot date or . . ."

"Listen to me. I'm trying to help you here. How about you help yourself for a change?"   She says nothing.

"You want to tell me what you were really doing tonight?"

Still she ignores him. Tongues her lip piercing.

"How are things with Januscz?"

And now she's looking at him. *Now* she's looking at him.

"What the fuck is that supposed to mean?"

Raw nerve.

"It's not supposed to mean anything."

"It's none of your fucking business. You're my parole officer not my fucking therapist." "Yes, I'm your parole officer. Which means that it's my responsibility to make sure you stick to the conditions of your parole, which in turn means I need to know that you are getting some stability in your life, not less."

He doesn't tell her that he's already checked up on Januscz, that he knows about the man's involvement in some of the island's chemical gangs, though admittedly as nothing more than one of their runt-runners.

"We're fine," she says, noncommittally.

Aleksakhina reaches into his pocket, holds up the vial and watches her demeanour change instantly. For a moment he thinks she is about to try to snatch the thing afterward.

"What were you doing with this?" he asks her.

Katja, her face is firm, stoic. He can tell she is trying hard to not give anything away.

"Where did you get it?" The liquid inside the vial is an almost golden colour under the starkness of the streetlight overhead.

"Did Januscz give this to you?"

"I don't have to answer these questions."

"I'm giving you a chance here, Katja. It doesn't have to be me asking these questions. But I don't want to have to take you in."

"Don't act like you're doing me a favour. You just don't want to deal with the paperwork. Come on, man! I haven't done anything. I just forgot to check in, that's all. Give me a fucking break here. I need to get out for my shift. I need that job! You're the one that's saying you want to see me get more stability in my life—how the fuck am I meant to do that if I lose my job?"

"I told you already, I'll talk with your boss."

"He won't give a shit. You think he'll even think twice about firing someone like me?"

"He will if I ask him not to. Now, I ask again—what is this and where did you get it?"

She crosses her arms, switches off. That's as much as he's going to get from her.

"Okay have it your way, Katja. You want to spend a night inside, be my guest. We'll talk again in the morning."

She kicks out at the back of the driver's seat in frustration as he turns away again.

"I found it, okay?! Jesus. I don't know where it came from. One of the customers at the diner left it behind."

"I thought you hadn't started your shift yet?"

"Yesterday," she says quickly. "I found it yesterday. They didn't leave a tip so I figured it would even us out. I don't know what the hell is even in there. I was going to see if Januscz knew someone who would. Maybe see if it was worth something."

And she almost convinces him with the story. Almost.

"Do you know what this means?" he asks her, tilting the

vial toward her so the watermark on the glass shows up. She shrugs and perhaps she really doesn't know or maybe she's just not saying.

Aleksakhina knows what it means, however.

End of conversation.

"Fine. We'll go to the station and I'll be back in the morning. Maybe you'll be more talkative then?"

She looks less controlled now, her desperation leaking through, and he lets the sentiment linger to give her one final chance to talk, but she doesn't. He finds himself grateful for her silence because he has no intention of sitting in the quickly cooling car for much longer, while trying to wring information out of her that might be a dead end anyway.

He starts the engine, drags the complaining vehicle through the ghostly night traffic. Before he reaches the station, however, he suddenly jerks the wheel and pulls over again.

"Wait here," he tells Katja, and he stalks across to a callbox daubed with bright yellow spray paint. He keeps one eye on the girl as he lifts the receiver, and is glad to hear a tone when he puts it to his ear.

He taps in the beginnings of a number. Stops.

Puts the phone down.

Picks it up, dials the number and finishes it this time.

"It's me," he says. "Nothing's the matter. I know I said I wouldn't call but . . . I just wanted to hear your voice. I can't talk for long. She's not here. No, I'm out. At work. Nothing, really. I just needed a break. Yes, I know. I miss you too."

And he says, "Goodbye," but the line is already dead.

He stands there for another few minutes and then takes out the vial, examines the watermark. He isn't well-versed enough to know which of the dealers' marks it is but it won't take too much effort to find out.

He walks back to the car feeling, for some reason, worse than before he made the call. Colder.

He knows he should go home.

But he stops, returns to the phone, dials another number, which this time he has to look up first. It's written in a notepad with no name or other means of identification beside it and the pad is filled with other numbers and addresses.

"It's Anatoli," he says when the connection is made. He avoids the use of his second name. "Oh. Will he be long? I see. No . . . I have something I'd like to show him. Something he might be interested in. Perhaps I should wait until I can speak to him. . . . Yes. Tonight, if possible. Yes. Thank you."

He puts the phone down, rolls the vial between his fingers. Katja is staring at him now through the rear window of his car, watches him all the way until he gets in.

"What's going on?" she asks suspiciously.

"Nothing, I just needed to make a few calls."

"Calls to who?"

"Nothing you need concern yourself with."

"So you're taking me in now?"

"Soon," he tells her. "I have to meet with someone first. You don't have any other plans do you?"

Katja sneers.

"Let's just get this over with," she says.

PART FOUR
KOHL

CHAPTER TWELVE

The thing is, when you're summoned by Szerynski, you go to him. You don't really have a choice in the matter. There is no, "Maybe later." There is no "I can't, I'm busy." And there is certainly no "Fuck off, I've got better things to do be doing with my time."

There is only:

"Yes, Mr. Szerynski."

So Kohl, that's what he says, into the phone.

"Yes, Mr. Szerynski."

And when he presses a button to hang up the phone, he adds this:

"Fuck."

Then he picks up the phone again and puts it to his ear. He wants to make sure he hung it up properly and that Szerynski didn't hear that last comment.

The line is dead.

He hits the on/off button just to make sure. Static hums in his ears and there is no Szerynski.

He checks once more, just to be absolutely certain.

Spread out across the table before him are dozens, if not hundreds, of little pieces of metal and plastic. There are coils, springs, washers, and ball bearings. There are round knobs and angular ones. There are little spikes and there are rods of varying length. Most of them are scattered around the surface but there are some that he's already arranged into neat piles. He's categorizing them by size and type and material, having emptied them from the dozens of little drawers of the cabinet that stores them. They were already organized before he took them out but he performs this procedure every once in a while anyway.

It calms him.

He moves the coils to one side, separates them out depending on size, but then he finds that there are some of different size to every other coil there and that will not do. He needs even numbers. That's what makes sense.

Odd numbers are . . . odd.

He shoves all the coils back into the main pile, losing them again to the other pieces of metal. Decides he will need to find another method of organization.

Weight?

Shape?

Reflectivity?

Something that will fit them all into place. Something that will make sense.

But there's no time, Szerynski has summoned him. He must go.

He tightens the red-tinted goggles over his glaucoma-shot eyes, then quickly pushes all the fragments on the table into a single pile in the middle. He adjusts the pile minutely until it is as close to a perfect circle as he can manage, pokes the final few pieces that stick out.

It will have to do.

He puts on an old biker jacket, the symbols and patches of which have become worn and tattered, tells Misha that he is going out for a while. She is stretched out on the couch in the hallway, her oiled and muscled legs draped over the couch's arm as she performs crunching sit-ups. Grunts at him.

Szerynski's hole is ten blocks away and by the time Kohl gets there, his legs are wet up to the calves from the rainwater puddling the streets. The hole is actually a multi-storey garage with automated shutters instead of doors, and instead of windows, hatches large enough to crane cars out of. Automobile corpses are stacked three high on either side of the entrance and Kohl knows from past experience that Szerynski will have one of his men hidden in them.

He hits a buzzer and a moment later a shutter is opened at eye level and then there is the painful grinding sound of the door being opened.

The man who greets Kohl is like a bagful of meat. He probably once had a firm, muscular figure but for whatever reason his body has relaxed now, giving the effect of a melting sculpture.

"My name is Vladimir Kohl. I'm here to see Mr. Szerynski. He is expecting me."

And as he is led inside, Kohl finds himself thinking about the pile of arcade machine pieces lying on his workbench. He thinks of the errant pieces that stick out at the sides and feels a desperate need to return and fix them.

"This way."

Melting Man leads Kohl through the expansive room the door opens onto, obviously the main work area back when the place was still a working garage. The ramps that would have once jacked the cars up so engineers could look at their undersides remain in place and a number of pale, spidery-limbed girls and boys are variously leaning and lying on them.

Kohl ascends a metal staircase to the second floor, watching the way the Melting Man's flesh moves hypnotically with each step.

He thinks of little pins and screws. Of curved and L-shaped edgings. Of hexagonal mouldings. And if he just keeps thinking of these, he won't think about why Szerynski has summoned him there and what it might mean.

He hears the sound of chains as they approach the doorway to another workshop, of chains clanking together as if something wrapped within them is moving. He hesitates when a groan emerges from within and the Melting Man turns to him with a grin on his jiggling face. The grin says, I know you don't want to go in there and I know you realize you have to.

Kohl is shoved inside and the smell of spices washes

over him. There are about a dozen people gathered inside, mostly milling around in small groups next to an oil drum burning cool, green flames. The room is as tall as those downstairs, and he realizes the clanking sounds are coming from a pulley system of some sort being tended to by a couple of bare-chested, tattooed men.

Kohl is led to the other side of the shadowy room, to a medical gurney partially surrounded by a dirty plastic screen. Szerynski is naked and laid out on the table on his stomach. A woman in a tight white latex uniform stands behind him, a two-inch hook in one hand and a wad of red-stained cotton in the other.

Szerynski looks up, notices Kohl and fixes his eyes upon the other man.

The woman in latex rubs a point on Szerynski's back with the cotton, smearing the dark substance Kohl takes to be iodine. Then she pinches his skin between her thumb and forefinger, shoves the hook into it and it stretches the skin for a moment before popping and the hook goes straight through him.

Szerynski barely flinches, just keeps looking directly into Kohl's eyes.

Then he says, "Kohl."

As if they're just sitting around in his office or one of his labs. As if he's not lying there with six hooks perforating him along either side of his spinal column.

As if this was normal.

Kohl tries to play along.

"I was told you wanted to see me."

"Indeed."

Szerynski flinches a little as another hook punctures him, this time farther out toward his shoulder, where his deltoids meet his infraspinatus muscles. Little tears of blood trickle across his skin, weeping for him because he will not.

Kohl's fingers are entwined. He's trying to fight back the anxiety caused by the open wounds, fresh blood, and rusted metal. He thinks he hears bugs or rats in the walls.

Half-inch washers. Three-quarter-inch ones.

Arrange the coils according to age, not size. How will he know how old they are? So according to their condition, then.

No, too subjective.

"Kohl."

And Kohl snaps himself out of his daydream. Szerynski is waving him to one side, the latex nurse standing behind the gurney now. Kohl steps aside and she pushes the prostrate, punctured man past and toward the gurney the tattooed men are still working on.

The rest of them, the others gathered there, are turning now, preparing themselves for what is to come.

Kohl's stomach clenches.

He goes to Szerynski's side once more and wonders if this is some sort of twisted warning.

"I have some information," Szerynski tells him as he is swung around on the bed. The tattooed men pull on the chains and Kohl sees sturdy metal loops on the end. "Dracyev is onto something new. He's cooked it up already."

One of the men pulls the nearest hook up toward the metal loop he holds in one hand, stretching Szerynski's skin out several inches until it is spread thin enough that Kohl can see the blood pumping through the veins within. Szerynski grimaces and another trickle of blood begins and then he is hooked into the first loop.

"He's getting one of his mules to take it to the mainland tonight. He'll be travelling on a cargo ship at midnight."

A second hook is latched onto a loop. The skin remains stretched because the chains don't come all the way down. It looks like little volcanoes of flesh erupting along the chemist-dealer's back.

"I want you to intercept the man before he can get there. Take the chemical from him using whatever means necessary."

Another hook, another.

Szerynski's features contort. When they soften once more he says, "You understand?"

"Dracyev?" Kohl says. "I'm not . . ."

"Not what?" Szerynski asks. "Not one of my employees? Not bothered about pissing me off and returning to being the fucking useless junkie you were when I first met you? Not what, Vladimir?"

"Nothing."

A high-pitched humming sounds and the chains begin to tighten. They are being slowly, slowly dragged toward the ceiling and soon, therefore, will Szerynski.

"I ask you a favour and I give you a reward, is that not my way?"

And his words are almost drowned out by the sound of the machinery and the excited gasps of the gathered crowd—most of whom, Kohl notes, are young women.

"Yes," Kohl says weakly.

"Good. If you do this for me then I will find a position for you which will reward you justly."

Kohl stands and watches as Szerynski drifts toward the ceiling, suspended from the eight hooks poking out of his skin like parasitic worms, vanishing into the darkness above.

uck that.

He's not going to get stuck in the middle of any gang rivalry. Szerynski has been good to him in his own unique way but Kohl knows where his limits lie. He knows what can happen when you start dicking around with other dealers; he's seen the results himself.

He's back in his workshop and he's finished organizing the washers and coils and other miscellanea and neatly put them back into the little drawers in the cabinet and he's not feeling any better for it. The world doesn't make any more sense. Size and shape and material. Everything just blurring at the edges, chaos.

He picks up a fragged circuit board that has been pulled out of a battered cabinet he doubts will ever return to the floor. He can see where the solder lines that bus the game's information from one chip to another have cracked and so grabs his blowtorch and fires it up.

Distraction.

Deviation.

And the buzzer goes—the buzzer that's connected to the booth downstairs where Fat Rita sits for sixteen hours a day in return for as much coffee and cans of processed food as she can handle.

He ignores it at first but it goes again and so he answers and it's Rita because it's always Rita and Rita tells him that one of his customers is here to see him and the rest, the rest has already been told.

So skip forward to Kohl, pinning the useless fucking junkie, pinning Nikolai, to the wall with the blowtorch looming in his face like an angry serpent.

The junkie has been unlucky enough to catch Kohl at this awkward moment and Kohl has exploded in the man's face as the circuit boards do from time to time, taking his money, fucking him over just because he can, because he's feeling fucked over by Szerynski. He's taking it out on Nikolai as if he can encourage some sort of transference that will rid him of the problem of Szerynski's offer.

His instruction.

He lets the torch bring hundreds of little marbles of sweat to Nikolai's brow, then sweeps it across his neck.

"If you ever want me to even consider selling you or any of your junkie friends anything ever again then you'll do what's good for you and get the fuck out of my joint right now."

The junkie seems confused by Kohl's gentle tones and so the chemical dealer sweeps the torch across Nikolai's throat once more.

Kohl shouts for Misha and the woman barges in, hooks Nikolai cleanly and catches him before he falls to the ground. She holds him up so Kohl can sneer into his face.

"You bring me the rest of what you owe me by tomorrow night, Nikolai. Then we can talk further."

And then Misha drags the little piece of shit away and the door slams shut and Kohl slumps back into his seat.

And it's not until later that he realizes how stupid he has been.

But he does realize, eventually, as he's still sitting in his workshop stewing over being forced into helping Szerynski when all he wants is for his life to be calm, controlled, ordered. To make sense.

He realizes that there's no need to risk anything at all.

Szerynski wants the vial. He wants Kohl to get it for him.

He didn't specify, however, that it should be Kohl personally, who gets it.

Szerynski is getting Kohl to do his dirty work so why shouldn't Kohl do the same? Dog eats dog eats dog eats dog and so on, and Kohl says to himself, as he walks away from Nikolai's run-down apartment building: "A place for everything and everything in its place."

Nikolai, he realizes, has his place.

The joystick junkie fitted neatly into the socket Szerynski created, as easily as a lithium ion battery would clip into the motherboard of a games cabinet.

So Kohl, he's back at the arcade now but not hidden away in his workshop, instead knee-deep in pixel-air and gamer-shouts. Bathing in the buzz generated by a room full of spaced-out kids and groggy old timers who can no longer play because their fingers have become too gnarled.

Many know who Kohl is, many don't. But he's not after recognition.

The glow of the machines bleeds into the air before him, a strange side effect of the goggles he wears, and at times he is walking through these colourful tides and swears he feels them wash over him. And he is smiling because he is thinking about Nikolai bringing him the vial in return for a pittance of product, risking his itching junkie neck for a couple of hits.

And he is thinking about then calling Szerynski and giving the vial to him and in return getting whatever reward the chemical lord has in mind with little real risk to Kohl himself.

And he is thinking about rearranging the cabinets sometime soon, giving them a fresh sense of order, organizing them by height or age or game-play style.

He sits on the ledge created by the high backs of the booth seats, watching the gamers, listening to the cries of joy and annoyance and waiting, just waiting for Nikolai to come back to him with the vial, and he has no idea how wrong things are about to go.

PART FOUR
BEFORE THINGS WENT WRONG

CHAPTER FOURTEEN

He uses the tattoos as guides and presses the end of the scalpel blade into his skin where the design curves from one tribal spike to another. Drags the blade along the arc, drawing a line of blood that rises through the cut and chases the implement like fire running along a kerosene trail.

He pauses, wipes the blood away, then starts again at another part of the design. He's in lab 34, one of the smaller rooms toward the back of the complex and away from the permanent partying that takes place in the main warehouse where he would, later that night, put on a display of either suspension or kavadi. It will depend on how he feels nearer the time.

The room is dark, save for the surgical light he points down at his arm, laid out upon an empty instrument tray.

He wipes away new blood as it rises to the surface, then with his free hand picks up a bottle of India ink and offers it to the girl sitting on the worktop beside him.

She's made a vague attempt at putting her clothes back on after that afternoon's activities but looks as if she got bored after a few minutes or perhaps hadn't had full control of her limbs. She's missed one of the arm straps of her t-shirt and one of her stockings has slouched back down to calf-level, like a half-shed skin. She doesn't notice Szerynski offering her the ink bottle because she's too busy examining the fresh, wet welts left by the ropes he had used on her.

"Open this," he says to get her attention.

She hops off the worktop and the stocking tumbles to her ankle. She opens the bottle for him and places it back down on the instrument tray. His blood, meanwhile, is making patterns like the scrawl of some ancient language upon his skin. She leans into the light for a closer look.

Szerynski wipes the blood away again then touches the index finger of his free hand to the ink. Pauses.

"What you told me earlier, you heard this from Dracyev yourself?" he asks the girl.

She says *yeah* distractedly. She's watching the ink droplet gathering on the tip of his finger, precariously held there by surface tension alone, lingering over the fresh cuts.

"You fucked him?"

"Yeah." Distractedly again. "Are you going to . . . ?"

"In a minute. You're sure it's tonight? The courier is taking it to the mainland tonight?"

"Yes."

The droplet is stretching now, straining against the laws of physics, as if desperate to plunge into the wound itself.

"Tonight. A guy called . . . called . . . shit . . ."

And she tries to remember quickly, wanting him to just get on with it.

". . . Januscz. I don't know his second name. He's just a runner."

"Why would Dracyev pick him to take it? If it's as important to him as you said . . ."

"I don't know. Maybe because he's disposable."

"Everyone's disposable."

And Szerynski suddenly hisses as the ink drops into one of the fresh cuts. He presses his finger down and rubs the ink along the groove of the opened flesh, working it in deeply, and it feels like hydrochloric acid because of the way it burns. His arm shakes with pain and so he concentrates on swallowing the sensation, drawing it into himself.

His eyes close and in his mind is whitespace. Nothingness.

He opens his eyes again and the girl, she's still there, staring down at the wounds. The cuts would take about a week to heal, another week or so to scab off, and after that there would just be the thick clear lines of the ink rubbing.

He clears more blood from one of the other cuts, dips his finger in the ink again.

"Did he give you a time?"

"Nothing that specific," the girl says dreamily. She's entranced by his self-harm, his self-control. "He was just mouthing off, I think. Trying to impress me."

"And did he?"

"No," she says simply and quietly.

He presses the ink into the cut, works it along the wound's length and this time he's more ready for the pain and ducks away from it before it reaches him. It's a feeling of ascendance, one which he will experience to a greater degree later that night as he performs. At these times he feels as if he is growing, evolving. His body becoming a conduit.

He is aware of the ink being absorbed into his bloodstream, of the glare of the light and the girl reaching between his legs—but he doesn't experience any of it in the way that is normal.

The plan to hijack Dracyev's merchandise from the carrier is already fully formed in his head, though he has no recollection of working it out. He just knows what will be done and how.

Now all he needs is to get someone dumb enough and desperate enough to get the vial for him.

And he thinks of Vladimir Kohl.

nd he thinks of Vladimir Kohl again as the suspension chains dangle him thirty feet above the ground and the small crowd gathered below. He thinks back to when the man was just another junkie lining up outside the very first arcade Szerynski opened, before he had expanded to over a dozen of them scattered across the island. When Kohl had come back night after night with those frazzled eyes of his exposed to the neon glows and electrical pulsing to get whatever he could with the measly funds he had managed to beg, borrow, or steal.

When Szerynski had seen the opportunity to wield Kohl's desperation to his own end and install him as one of the first who would deal out of his arcades.

The crowd below are caught between cheering as they would were they watching a band perform and silently appreciating as they would in an art gallery.

They don't know what Szerynski is and he likes that.

He closes his eyes and lets himself drift toward the whitespace again. It's a mother's womb and the calmness of suicide and more, but already it's starting to shiver and fade. It flickers like the last frames of an old movie and he concentrates on holding it steady but it moves, it moves in his grasp and he knows he can't hold it if he has to think about it so he stops thinking and then it slips further.

And he fluctuates like this for some time, bobbing up and down on the tide of some great white ocean that refuses to swallow him or spit him out.

He thinks perhaps he will stay there until Kohl arrives with the vial.

CHAPTER SIXTEEN

Бut eventually the undulations cease and he is broken from the moment by a grating, cranking sound. It takes him time to realize it is the noise of the pulleys working.

He is being lowered to the ground once more.

It must be over.

The crowd, for the most part, has waned, although he has no idea how long he has been suspended up there. What is left of those gathered regard him with only a vague interest and it seems as if they've forgotten why they came.

What exactly had they been expecting to see? Szerynski wonders.

His body aches all over except for the points where the hooks puncture his skin.

In these places there is a certain numbness, a dullness

void of feeling or unfeeling, and even as he presses his finger against them, there is no response. Mina, his fetish nurse, helps him onto a gurney and checks over his wounds with disinterest.

He feels as if he has lost something vital to his very being and she knows this.

"How long was I up there for?" he asks her.

"Three hours," she tells him. "Just like you asked."

"Are you sure? I wasn't brought down early?"

She takes out the hooks one by one. Squeezes congealed blood from them.

"You ask for three hours, you are up there for three hours. You did not get anywhere?"

Neither of them know where it was he had been heading but wherever it was, he hasn't made it yet again.

"No," he snaps.

Mina removes the final hook with a satisfying pop from the stretched skin and Szerynski sits up.

"We'll try it again in two nights," he says, and Mina doesn't respond.

She has left him, walked off into the darkness at the edges of the room, her job complete for the night.

Szerynski remains on the gurney, his legs dangling into the darkness below him, and for several moments he is captured by the intense feeling that if he were to drop himself down into it he would fall forever.

He looks up when someone emerges from the shadows of the now-silent room.

This man, Drago, is thick and full of meat like an

overstuffed sausage. His fingers flex nervously as he stands before the naked chemical lord. He is holding a robe.

Szerynski steps into the garment and walks away without saying anything. Stops when Drago tells him that someone has been trying to contact him on his private line.

"Who was it?" Szerynski demands irritably. He is aware of the stigmata tears of blood trickling from each of his wounds.

Drago tells him, keeping a certain distance between himself and Szerynski.

"What did he want?"

"He wouldn't say, specifically. Wanted to talk to you. Tonight." Szerynski isn't in the mood for that. Isn't in the mood for anything now.

"I'm going to Czechmate," he tells Drago, striding past him, the robe flowing in his wake.

"What if he calls again?" Drago says.

But Szerynski is already through the door and doesn't slow his pace until he reaches his personal quarters on the third floor. He changes quickly, feels little jolts of numb-pain where his clothes brush against the fresh wounds.

It's a seven-block walk to the arcade and his pace doesn't falter once the entire length of the journey. He avoids the fetish pull of the street girls whose eyes and posture seem to be filled with the glitter-sparkle of the stars above, whose boney hook-nailed fingers try to latch onto him as he passes.

He isn't in the mood.

The arcade is cold and dead when he reaches it, the

corrugated shutters rolled down over the entrance and the gas in the neon signage whispering gently through the glass tubing. He unlocks the side entrances and steps inside.

The air retains a constant electric charge like the pinhead of a great lightning storm, and if he hadn't shaved himself clean several days earlier his body hairs would now be standing on end. It is a familiar, god-like aura.

Most of the cabinets are shut down, but a few remain switched on, glowing morosely amongst their dormant fellows. These ones are the old faithful, the ones whose electronics are so fragile it would be too great a risk to switch them off for fear they might never return to life again.

He only opens the place occasionally now, when the inclination takes him.

For the most part, this is his personal zone, his own scratched and battered version of the whitespace he knows awaits him elsewhere. He wanders amongst the cabinets, running his hands across their dusty surfaces like a shopkeeper surveying the wreckage of his store after riots.

He stands before a machine that scrolls through a series of animations intermingled with lists of the top scores, and as he places his hands on the controls he feels a vibration at the back of his leg.

He pulls out his pager and reads the message scrolling across the LCD display. Hesitates with the device held in mid-air, about to be launched toward the room's opposite wall.

Something makes him stop and read again.

KATJA FROM THE PUNK BAND

Instead of destroying the pager, he taps in the number to a payphone that has been rigged with a piece of aluminum that tricks it into thinking coins have been fed into it.

"What do you want?" he says, his voice thick and flat. "Sorry, I'm not interested. If you . . . a what?"

His voice changes. His posture changes.

The hum of the machines fills his ears.

"Where did you get it?" He says this slowly, deliberately. He is silent for several moments and the voice on the other end says *hello*? To check that he is still there. "Bring it over. I'm at the Czechmate arcade, it's on . . . yes that's the one. Okay. I'll be waiting for you."

And the line goes dead but he doesn't put down the phone, not yet. The static hisses in his head and he has the feeling he used to get when he was still just a street-dealer passing out whatever chemicals he could get his hands on to whomever might want them. It's the feeling that a pickpocket gets when he realizes he's just snatched the wallet of an undercover cop, that a hooker gets when she's lead into an alley before things turn nasty, that an addict gets the moment they inject bad gear into their veins.

But he swallows his suspicions for now, plays a couple of games of a sideways-scroller until he hears the sound of a car pulling up outside. He goes to one of the building's few windows, peers around the piece of black plastic that covers the glass, and watches a man in a long dark coat walking nervously up toward the front door. Szerynski is still trying to figure out whether the shape in the back of the car is human when there is a knock.

He has a gun tucked into his waistband, a knife slotted into a sheath on his calf.

He opens the door and lets the man in.

"Thank you for seeing me."

"You have it with you?" Szerynski asks.

The man shifts nervously and Szerynski senses the man suddenly realizing the risk of bringing the object in question with him, but it's too late now.

"Let me see it."

Again the man hesitates. Control. They all want control of situations.

"If I'd have been interested in killing you for it, I would have already done so," Szerynski tells him flatly. "I've been good enough to spare you a moment of my time, the least you can do is show me what you have contacted me about."

Reluctantly the man reaches into his pocket, and when he brings out the vial, Szerynski's jaw flexes visibly. The dealer opens his palm and stares at it until the vial is placed there.

He tilts his hand and rolls it, then flicks on a lamp that hovers above a row of booths running along the near wall. He tilts the vial until the watermark reveals itself.

"You got this from a contact, you said?"

"Yes."

"His name?"

"Her," the man says, then seems to catch himself. "I can't give you that information."

"I see."

And Szerynski, he goes into his back pocket, fishes out a

KATJA FROM THE PUNK BAND

little pen-like device, flashes it across the vial.

"Where did they get it from?"

"I don't know. Look, is it worth something to you? Because if you don't want it, I can—"

"Don't be dramatic," Szerynski tells the man. "How much do you want for it?" And he sees the man quickly calculating how much he thinks he can wrangle from the dealer, but this doesn't matter, this doesn't interest him.

The man feeds him an amount and Szerynski smiles just for the sake of it. He has triple that in the arcade's small safe and the only reason it's in there is that it isn't worth the effort of getting it transferred to the vault back at his warehouse.

The dealer cuts ten grand from the amount for no good reason and the man agrees only too eagerly. Szerynski tells him to follow and together they go to the office that is practically stapled to the rear wall—a simple timber frame lined with sheet metal that chills the room.

He opens the safe and removes the entire stack of notes within, dumping them on the table for the man to see.

Szerynski separates the agreed amount, then holds another 30 Gs over it, ready to drop in with the rest.

"You sure you don't want to tell me where you got this?"

The man licks his lips, a subconscious and utterly primal gesture that makes Szerynski smile. He stares at the wad of notes for a few moments, closes his eyes, then shakes his head.

Then the man takes the money, as if it will disappear as some sort of knock-on effect of his refusal. He seems unsure what to do with it at first, then shoves it into his jacket pocket.

"If you change your mind," Szerynski says. "You have my number."

The man nods. Leaves.

Szerynski stares down at the notes still scattered across his desk, sits down in a chair that creaks with neglect. He examines the vial once more, his eyes lingering on Dracyev's seal imprinted on its glass.

Something is obviously going on. Something fucked up.

He will not be played with.

Kohl is up to something.

He ponders his options for a time and then finally picks up the phone. He dials the number of Kohl's arcade and a woman with a voice like sludge answers.

"He's not here," she says. "What do you want?"

Szerynski smiles at the fact she is being as rude to him as any other punter who might be calling up, not realizing that without him, there would be no Digital Drive-by. Not realizing that her job was just a sham, an excuse to get people in and out.

"Where did he go? When?"

"Look, who is this? If it's so fucking important then why don't you move your lazy ass and come down here? I've got better things to be doing with my time than . . ."

Her voice fades suddenly and Szerynski hears her barking at a customer in the background.

"Look, I've got work to do," she says, voice back to its full, searing clarity. "You want to leave a message or

101

something?"

"Just tell him that Mr. Szerynski wants to speak to him."

"Mr. Whuh?"

"Szerynski. S-Z-E . . ."

"Oh . . . wait. Waitaminute. Here he comes."

Her voice fades again and there are a few moments of shuffling noises.

"Mr. Szerynski."

Kohl's voice.

"Vladimir."

"I'm glad you called," the man says, sounding genuinely relieved. "Very good timing."

"Really," Szerynski replies cautiously. "Why's that?"

"Because I have your vial. I have it right here in my hands."

Szerynski sits forward in his seat. "You have the vial."

"No problems, Mr. Szerynski . No problems at all."

Szerynski's eyes fix on the vial on the desk before him.

"Then why don't you come right over, Vladimir. I'm eager to see you."

PART FIVE
KATJA AGAIN

CHAPTER SEVENTEEN

*S*TUCK IN THE BACK OF THE FUCKING CAR!!!!

How long now?

How long has it been?

She's sitting there silently fuming, hands clenched together, staring at the wire mesh that keeps her caged in there, as if the cuffs aren't bad enough. Her arm is throbbing from the constant battering she's received from her guitar, which now lies up against the opposite door, innocent of all charges.

Aleksakhina is outside, leaning over a callbox daubed with bright yellow spray paint. She watches him put the phone down, then he looks for a moment as if he is about to return to the car. Changes his mind. Taps in another number.

"What the fuck are you doing?" she says aloud through

gritted teeth.

She leans forward, checks the driver's area for the vial but she already knows he took it with him. Of all the nights for him to decide to lose his patience with her . . .

She's flexing her toes inside her boots. She glances at the clock on the dashboard.

Soon the boat will be preparing the leave the bay with its special passenger aboard, Januscz's perfect escape all ready and waiting for her. And here she is, trapped in the back of a psycho parole officer's creaking, rusted car, unable to do anything about it.

She peers through the mesh at the analog clock, the arms of which are quickly working their way around the dial.

Leans forward and scans the foot wells for something, anything.

The floor is littered with a spray of sugar like cut glass, like fallen stars.

She rolls onto her side and sees something in the shadows of the passenger's seat. It's an effort to contort herself into a position where she can reach out to it with her hands still cuffed behind her back, but she manages it. She stretches out blindly behind her toward where the object had been, and a burning begins in her shoulder but she ignores it, reaches farther, fingertips scraping across the dirty carpet, and the she feels something, grips it between forefinger and second finger.

She twists back out again, checks that Aleksakhina is still on the phone. She drops the object onto the seat beside her and turns to see that it is a cigarette butt, almost snapped clean in half but not quite.

There's a moment of disappointment but her mind is still working and the moment is gone. A match. She needs a match—or a lighter.

She manages to reach into her back pocket and take out her lighter. More contortions, then the cigarette butt is lit and she turns, twists, drops it through onto the driver's seat. It just sits there for a moment and she panics that it's going to die out, then there's a little burst of light and the seat's fabric has caught fire.

The flames flicker then rise quickly toward her, small vents of heat brushing over her face. She smells the ugly chemical scent of the manmade materials burning and pulls herself away from the front of the car.

Glances at Aleksakhina and he's finishing his conversation, puts the phone back down. He's walking toward her but he's calm.

And he's calm because there is no fire. She has no lighter.

There is no escape.

The cigarette butt is beside her. It's like a little insect grub and she flicks it away in disgust.

Aleksakhina looks at her suspiciously as he climbs in, and for a moment she wonders if perhaps it isn't fantasy and there really is a fire.

Then he sits down, straightens his coat. "Everything okay back there?"

"Just peachy. What's going on?" she asks.

"Nothing, I just needed to make a few calls."

"Calls to who?"

"Nothing you need concern yourself with."

"So you're taking me in now?"

"Soon," he tells her. "I have to meet with someone first. You don't have any other plans do you?"

Katja sneers.

"Let's just get this over with," she says and he pulls out in front of a muscle car that has a glowing rim on its underside to give it the appearance of floating on a plate of blue light as it speeds around them. Bass-thumping music and testosterone aggression.

And she reminds herself—the longer she's in the car, the longer she's not in a cell, and the longer she still has a chance of making the boat.

For now—patience.

CHAPTER EIGHTEEN

And it's not long before he stops the car again, pulling it over when the glow of splintered neon comes into view ahead.

Katja's ready this time, concentrating, watching for the vial, and there it is, he plucks it from his pocket and grips it gently in his palm.

He turns to her, says, "Wait here. I won't be long."

"I need to go the bathroom," she tells him.

He ignores her, gets out of the car.

"If you leave me, I'm going to fucking piss myself here!" she shouts, but the door is slammed shut and it blasts through her words.

"Hey, come on! These cuffs are fucking . . . just give me a break!"

He doesn't hear or he isn't listening and he's got the vial

and he's walking away with her ticket off the island. Again.

She suddenly lashes out in anger, slamming her booted feet into the mesh in front of her again and again but she's been in the back of these types of vehicles enough to know they're easily strong enough to withstand such an attack. When she's done, she sees Aleksakhina disappear under a set of shutters that have been lifted open halfway by some sort of hydraulic system.

The place is an arcade but the garish lights that would normally scream out at anyone nearby are all dead so she can't read the signage. They could be anywhere. She looks around and the streets are deserted save for a handful of lurking figures, street ghosts and memories.

Claustrophobia presses in on her and she becomes increasingly aware of the bulk of the guitar still behind her. Moonlight gleams on the coils of excess strings that curl around the head of the instrument, a gentle strobe that calls her attention.

She shoves the thing with her thigh and then lets it topple over behind her so that it lies flat across the seat, then she shuffles toward the stray wires. She takes one between thumb and forefinger, holding it tight because it threatens to pull into a tight coil once more, and works it toward the keyhole of the cuffs. It's like trying to thread a needle blind.

Her fingers feel numb and she stabs herself, drops the wire.

Grits her teeth, takes another one, this one finer than the last.

She manages to slot it into the gap, conscious of the garage-style door Aleksakhina went through moments before. She rummages around in the metal chamber, waiting, just waiting for the solid click that will signal her release but it's not coming, it's not coming. Tongues her lip ring with concentration.

The wire slips again and she hears a noise somewhere outside, metal hitting metal.

Looks around.

Nothing.

"Come on."

And the string connects with something, she twists, twists again, and clunk. For a moment she is unable to move, afraid that whatever progress she might have made will be undone. Then slowly, slowly, she withdraws the wire and lifts her hands behind her back.

The cuff she has been working on falls away from her like an opened shell.

She holds it up in front of her as if to verify that she's actually managed it and there it is, dangling from her left wrist, her triumph. She uses the same string to unlock the sister cuff.

Now what?

Now wait for Aleksakhina to come back, arms behind her back as if nothing is wrong. Fake throat pains, maybe even work her vocal cords a little until blood comes, anything to get him to open the door for her.

The guitar neck in her hand.

And a swing like she often did while performing,

circling the thing around like a cruel hunter with a dead rabbit, crashing into the back of his head, just enough to floor him.

Then she will be gone.

But what about the vial?

The vial. The fucking vial.

Aleksakhina had taken it inside with him, but had it only been to keep it away from her? What had that phone call been about?

Fuck it, he was up to something.

And as this thought occurs to her, as before, she hears a noise from somewhere close by. She sees something moving in the rearview mirror and a darkness filters over her.

A feeling she has felt previously, just before something bad was about to happen.

When Januscz first turned on her.

When one of her mother's boyfriends had made sure she'd be breathing through a straw for the rest of her life.

When she dropped a bad pill and realized the tingling at the back of her head wasn't as it should be.

Perhaps Aleksakhina hasn't brought her out to a quiet district in the middle of the night just because she happened to be in the back of his car when he had an errand to run.

She slips her hands behind her back once more, holding the opened cuffs. She touches her fingers to the solid, waxy neck of the guitar.

The figure is now only just visible at the very edge of the mirror but there is a reflection now against the side window, and it seems as if there might be two of them out there, though it could be a trick of the light.

Her breathing rasps through the trach. Snakes moving in dry grass.

She's listening to the sounds of the footsteps, slow and careful amongst the gentle raindrops, and so when the gunshot sounds, it almost deafens her—like the bullet has smashed through her skull and out the other side.

She jumps with fright, realizes that the bullet has blasted into the door beside her instead of her head, turns in time to see the figure raising the gun once more and she doesn't hesitate again.

She kicks out at the damaged door and it swings open, the lock shattered by one or other of the impacts, pushes her way out with no illusion of still being cuffed, pulls the guitar out behind her, but it's heavy and drags across the fabric of the rear seats. She's still pulling on it when she turns and sees the gun raised before her, ready to shoot, jerks hard on the instrument and screams as she would at the crescendo of one of her songs, swings the guitar around.

It connects at the exact same moment a second shot is fired and there is a cry of pain. The guitar's momentum carries her off balance and she staggers to one side, and the figure, the figure has slumped to its knees, holds its face. She raises the guitar a second time, ready to cleave it into the skull of her attacker.

CHAPTER NINETEEN

So apparently it's not easy trying to find a person in the middle of the night amidst an island full of people—who'd have thought it?

Nikolai, he's been rushing from one place to the next with no real idea of where to look. He's been to the club where he saw Katja's punk band perform just a few nights earlier, asked about her and her band mates but nobody knew anything, of course.

So where to look?

Was the man that had taken her another lover?

No, he seemed too official for that.

A friend or partner of some sort to Januscz?

Someone that had found the man's body and had come back for the vial? That had to be it.

A heavy from one of the drug lords.

When the realization hit him, he'd come close to turning his car around and going back to his apartment, fearful of what it might mean if he involved himself any further in this mess, but then he was already involved.

He's already up to his neck in it.

He's fucked over Vladimir Kohl and if the man hasn't already discovered what he has done then it's just a matter of time. He reminds himself—he needs to get off the island, and to get off the island he needs Katja.

It's as simple as that.

At least it's as simple as that until he finally spots the car—purely by chance and just as he's about to start hyperventilating with panic.

It's parked outside Czechmate, an arcade Nikolai has been to on occasion but not for a while.

An arcade that belongs to, and is personally run by, Wvladyslaw Szerynski.

The man that tells Kohl what to do and when.

"Oh, shit."

And there's that feeling again, the panic swelling up inside him and he just wants to run, to get away from all this. All he'd asked for was one more chance.

Now this.

But he can see her in the back of the car and her head moves—she's still alive.

He has to grab one of the paper bags he keeps in the glove compartment and shove it to his face until his spitfire breathing comes under control.

Opens the car door slowly, quietly. Picks up the gun that

lies on the passenger seat next to him, the gun Kohl gave him.

He moves carefully along the side of a nearby building, sticking to the shadows. He watches for signs of the man who has taken her but can't see anyone. It might be a trap.

If she's told them about him helping her, they might be deliberately luring him into something. Or maybe Kohl has found out about the fake vial.

His hands are shaking so much he can barely keep a hold of the gun.

Across the street, a pair of rent boys are talking to one another, crouched by a dumpster, picking through something on the pavement before them. They don't notice Nikolai as he makes his way toward the car, finally edging out onto the road since some of the bulbs in the streetlights are out. Gun in his quivering hand.

His eyes dart around like a hyperactive child's, just waiting for the moment when the ambush is revealed, but then he's within a few feet of the car and still nothing.

They must be inside, hiding beside her.

Waiting for him to open the door and reach in and then *wham*.

One dead Nikolai.

He tries to swallow but the saliva catches in his throat and he chokes momentarily.

He raises the gun a bit more, aims at the side of the car, toward the driver's side but below the window.

One shot. He'll fire one shot and either he'll hit them if they're hiding out there or it will stun them enough to give him time to grab Katja and/or split.

This is what it comes down to.

He just wants to go home.

Breathes once.

In.

Out.

Aiming, squinting past the blur of the tears in his eyes.

Fires.

The gun jumps more than he expects, but he hears the bullet impacting in one brief, high-pitched explosion. The recoil sends him stumbling to one side but he recovers quickly, snaps the gun up to eye level once more, ready for whatever might come.

One of the car doors opens but he's still too dazed to properly tell which, and his finger is squeezing on the trigger, but then something happens and everything goes insanely bright as if the arcade's lights have suddenly come to life. The side of his head is stirring with a strange heat and he's on his knees without any idea of how he got there.

There's a sound, a siren, but it's just in one ear, a screaming pain.

He turns and sees someone: it's Katja, Katja looming over him, swinging something in her hands.

He holds out a hand and shouts, "Wait!" but the word is faint and gurgling and so he tries to say it again.

His head swims, his movements slow and dragging as if he is underwater.

"I . . . uhhh . . ."

His tongue is fat and thick in his mouth.

His vision pulses, throbs, and he's aware of a small trail of saliva spilling out of the corner of his mouth.

"Nikolai?"

He's still holding his hand out to her, waving it at her blindly.

"Stop," he manages.

And then she's beside him and it's her guitar she had been wielding, now placed on the ground beside her.

"Jesus Christ, what the hell are you doing? Fucking *shooting* at me?"

"I . . . uuhhh . . ." Another pulse, another. "I thought it was a trap. . . . I thought they were waiting for me."

"Shit, are you okay? Your head . . ."

"It's okay," he tells her. "My throbs are just templing a little. I mean . . . am I bleeding?"

"Uhhhhh . . . yeah."

There is a gash across the side of his head from his brow line to his ear and it's glistening in the low light amidst the dark swathes of his hair. When he looks at Katja he isn't focusing properly on her.

"The man who took you . . . where . . . ?"

He tries to get to his feet, has to lean on Katja but he's scrawny enough that she can take his weight.

"He went inside the arcade."

"Arcade . . . ?"

The word doesn't make sense to him at first and he has to fight to understand it, but before he can manage it, there is a shout from somewhere nearby.

"It's him," Katja hisses and her grip on Nikolai softens.

He collapses again onto one knee.

"Get up!" she shouts, pulling him to his feet with one arm and grabbing her guitar with the other. It's a reflex action, one she's learned from dozens of hastily abandoned gigs, and she looks across at the entrance to the arcade as Aleksakhina comes out.

"Hey!" the man shouts, and he reaches into his jacket. Pulls out a weapon.

"Run!" Katja cries and she's pulling Nikolai along behind her, slings the guitar around her neck as she drags him toward the alleys that line the streets.

A shot is fired and it ricochets off a trash can, sending it spinning across the sidewalk in front of the two fugitives, almost taking Nikolai out. He stumbles across it and they vanish into the tiny gap between two stained, crumbling buildings.

Another shot rings out and they keep going, squeezing through the gap awkwardly, Nikolai unable to remain in a straight line for any length of time. Katja ducks into a doorway, pulls him in after her. Twists her guitar neck around and uses the same string she used to undo her cuffs to poke into the keyhole, and there's another clunk and she opens the door, steps to one side, pushes Nikolai through and he falls to the ground inside. She takes one last glance along the alley, thinks she sees a figure at the far end, follows Nikolai in, closes the door and leans against it.

Her throat is tight and burning from the exertion and she has to fight the urge to cough and clear out the trach tube. Nikolai is sprawled out beside her on the bare floor

117

like a chemical party leftover.

Through the heavy metal of the door, Katja listens for the sounds of Aleksakhina coming for them, but hears nothing. She coughs, unable to hold it back any longer, and for a few moments afterward is ready for the door to be kicked in behind her, but everything stays calm.

Calm.

"You okay?" she asks Nikolai finally because he's hardly moved.

"I can't," he says blearily. "Not right now."

"What? Are you okay?"

"Whuh?"

"Nikolai?"

She leaves the guitar leaning up against the door, moves across to him.

The flow of blood seems to have stopped and is clotting in his hair now. She checks the wound but there isn't much light in the place. A bruise is quickly forming next to his eye socket.

"Sit up," she tells him and he does so, with her help.

"How many fingers am I holding up?"

"How many whuh?" he asks.

"Fingers. Look at me. How many fingers? Can you see?"

"Three," he says without focusing properly.

"Look at them first."

"I am."

"Nikolai, I'm over here."

"Whuh? Oh."

"Shit."

She decides they'll need to stay for a short while at least; there is no way he'll properly keep up with her if they have to split now.

She looks around for the first time, and it's like some sort of workshop, but one that's not been used for some time. Metal shelving is pinned to most of the walls and the only window has been blacked out either deliberately or with the natural build-up of grease and dirt. Old machinery is mounted on racks, blades blunted and chains rusted.

There's a sink in one corner and she tries the taps but isn't surprised when nothing comes out. Finds a pile of old rags on a worktop and takes one, uses it to dab away some of the blood from Nikolai's face.

He watches her while she does it and his pupils seem more direct, more alive now.

"Feeling any better?"

"A little. At least there's only one of you now."

"Yeah, that's always a bonus." She dabs more blood away. "Look, I'm sorry for hitting you but you fucking shot at me, you know? What the fuck were you doing?"

"I thought they would be waiting for me. Using you to lure me out."

"They?"

"The chemical gang, the people that kidnapped you."

A faint, brief smile emerges on her face and he likes how it changes her into something softer.

"Chemical gang? Shit, no. That was no chemical gang."

"Oh." And he catches himself, as if something has become clear to him all of a sudden. "Uhhh . . . another

119

boyfriend?"

"Jesus, no. My parole officer. Aleksakhina." And she can't help but notice relief on his face.

"Oh. I . . . So what's he doing going into one of Szerynski's arcades at this time of night?"

"Who the fuck knows . . . wait . . . how do you know the place is Szerynski's?"

She's staring right at him, the trach tube wavering slightly, distractingly.

"I . . ."

A beat.

"I play. A little. Used to compete."

"You know the man?"

"Only by reputation. I mean, I've heard his name mentioned."

She takes these answers, considers them, stores them for later use.

"Whatever. He might be involved in this, then."

"Does it matter? We should just go, get out of here."

"We can't."

"Why not?"

"Aleksakhina. He took the vial."

A weight drops in Nikolai's chest. "You don't have it?"

She shakes her head.

"What did he take it for?"

"He's up to something. His type always are."

"So . . . what now?"

And he's intimately aware of how it's just the two of them, huddled in the middle of the old workshop. The sound of the rain is like a distant war that doesn't matter.

Katja drops the blood-stained cloth and gets up. Brushes aside some of the dirt from the window but it's still impossible to make anything out.

"Wait there."

And she opens the door slowly, carefully, leans her head out and steps through.

Checks the alley in both directions and goes back inside.

"Can you walk?" she asks Nikolai.

She reaches out, helps him to his feet and he staggers somewhat, steadies himself.

"I'm okay."

"Do you still have that gun?"

He has to think about it, then realizes he doesn't.

"I must have dunked it . . . dropped it . . . back at the cash. The car. I mean the car."

She gives him a pained look. "You sure you're okay?"

He nods, and instantly grimaces as pain shoots across his temples.

"I don't see anyone," Katja says, slinging her guitar across her back and around so that she wields the neck like a crowbar. "But be careful, okay?"

He nods and winces again.

Together they edge out into the alley, squinting through a light drizzle and the blurred streetlights. Nikolai has to use the sides of the buildings as support but manages to keep up with her. The pain is subsiding now.

Or maybe he's losing consciousness.

Katja holds him back as they reach the opening that

leads back out toward the arcade.

"Shit."

"What is it?"

"The car's gone. Aleksakhina's gone."

"My car?"

"You came in your car? Where?"

"I left it farther up the street there, next to a dumpster."

"I can't see from here."

"But Aleksakhina's car is gone? He's gone?"

"Looks like it."

"That's a good thing, isn't it?"

She turns, fixes him with a look that is one step away from a dirty uppercut.

"That means the vial is gone."

"Oh."

"Yes. Oh."

And she says, "Shouldn't have run. Goddamn. Should have just stood our ground, we could have had him. We had the gun."

The gun.

And she's running out toward the arcade now. Nikolai takes a few moments to comprehend this, then follows her. She's scanning the ground for the gun, pushing aside torn newspapers and pieces of trash, can't find it. Aleksakhina must have found it.

She looks around the neighbourhood as if for inspiration but none comes.

"What do we do now?" Nikolai asks. "Try and find him?"

"I guess," she answers, unconvincingly.

Without the gun, she thinks. Tightens her grip on the guitar for reassurance. Turns and takes another few paces toward the dead arcade. There is a concrete area out front, pieces of broken glass from vodka bottles, and lots of little shot glasses like the cogs of some translucent machine scattered around.

"Where are you going?"

But she doesn't listen to him, striding carefully between the debris so as to not make any noise, watching for signs of movement coming from within the darkness of the building. It seems somehow wrong, perverted, for a place of such energy and brightness to be so still.

Unnatural.

Her fingers absently squeeze the cold bulk of the guitar.

Nikolai is lurking somewhere behind her, half crouching as if trying to hide amidst nothing more than the acid atmosphere.

"We have to go inside," she tells him. "He was up to something in there. I want to know what."

The shutters are down across the entrance and there are no visible windows. She creeps around the side of the building, stops, motions at Nikolai.

"Are you coming or what?"

And he's about to answer when they both freeze—voices coming from inside.

Nikolai is still standing before the entrance when a gunshot rings out from inside. Katja ducks around the corner instinctively, drops to her knees. Another shot. Another.

There's a commotion, then a metallic tremble.

The shutters are being opened.

Katja calls to him but Nikolai, he seems stuck there. It's a fifty yard sprint to get back to the safety of the alleys they just came out of, more than that in any other direction.

"Get over here!" she shout-whispers.

There's a hand at the bottom of the shutters lifting them up and it sounds as if the pneumatics that operate the door aren't being used. The door is being forced open.

"Nikolai!"

He thinks of his machines back in the apartment, the electronic solace they offer, the pixel-heavy haven that's rescued him so many times. He thinks of pills and powders, spoons and straws.

"Nikolai!"

The shutters are open to knee-height now and the person opening them, they're scooting down to slide under.

And then something snaps inside Nikolai and he's moving, sprinting toward the side of the building where Katja waits in the shadows for him, an ice-white arm reaching out.

As he pushes himself in beside her, they hear footsteps crunching on broken glass, heavy breathing.

"Is that Szerynski?" she asks.

Nikolai peers around her cautiously.

The figure stumbles across the kerbing outside the arcade. Stops. Turns, perhaps to see if anyone is following, perhaps because he heard them in the alley.

Moonlight swirls around the fly-like glasses he wears.

The pair duck back into the shadows and Nikolai pins

Katja to the wall.

"Well?" she asks.

"It's not Szerynski," he tells her.

"So who the fuck is it?"

Swallows. "His name is Kohl. Vladimir Kohl."

CHAPTER TWENTY

Шho the hell is Vladimir Kohl?"

Snap-whispered as the man moves farther away, toward the glittering streetlights across the junction.

"He works for Szerynski," Nikolai says.

And he tenses, staring straight ahead, deliberately not meeting her eyes just in case she sees something there he's not ready for her to see.

How do you know him? Did he send you? You're after the vial, aren't you?

Swallows.

But she doesn't ask those questions—instead, another:

"What is he doing?"

They both watch as Kohl stops dead. Backtracks several paces, hesitates, then begins forward again. Looks down at his feet, stops. Waits for several moments then restarts his journey, this time without pause, all the way across the empty junction.

"We have to go after him," Katja says, and Nikolai has to grab her, pull her back toward him.

"No!"

"What do you mean, *no*? He could have the vial. What if some sort of deal has just gone down? He might have it."

"But . . ." And he can't think of a reason not to go after the man, at least not one that he can use. "But he might not."

"Well there's only one way to find out."

And she's getting up again, twisting in advance this time so that when Nikolai reaches for her he can't get a decent grip and she slips away from him, and he almost shouts to her with Kohl still in earshot, grabs the neck of her guitar and holds on.

Whisper-shouts, "Wait!"

"What is your fucking problem?!" And she really does shout and they both turn, look, expecting to see Kohl, looking back into the alley, gun in hand.

The gun. If they still had it, they could just fucking shoot him.

Just fucking shoot him and . . .

"He's gone," Katja says, straightens up. "For fuck's sake he's fucking gone, you moron."

She paces out to the very lip of the alley, but there're three ways the man could have gone and no way to know which he chose, or what might lie awaiting them in the darkness.

"I'm sorry, I just . . ."

Katja kicks out at the building's wall with a heavily booted foot, takes a chunk of brick out the size of her fist. Brings the guitar's heavy body around for another frustrated swipe but stops in mid-arc.

"There's still time, maybe we could . . ."

"He's gone," she says flatly.

Nikolai lingers, unsure of what to do or say next. He's still waiting for Kohl to step out of a shadow somewhere, weapon pointed at them and harbouring a serious desire to make Nikolai suffer for a very long time.

If he knew. If he'd already found out the vial was full of nothing but a few dozen millilitres of Nikolai's piss.

If.

"What are you doing?"

Katja, she's crouched by the arcade's shutter-door, examining the locking mechanism.

"This isn't locked. He didn't shut it properly."

She reaches under the metal frame and lifts it slowly, gently, and it moves with a great metal creak.

She winces at the volume of the sound, hesitates.

"We're going inside?" Nikolai whispers to her, crouching down.

"Of course we're going inside. I want to know what's going on with my fucking vial."

And again there's that sensation of wanting to run, to just get out of the whole situation and take his chances with whatever Kohl might have planned for him, but then there's Katja and she's like a strong current that doesn't realize or care that she's dragging him along with her.

She's already opened the door enough to slide underneath, first checking inside to make sure it's safe. Nikolai feels an urge to insist he goes first, but he doesn't know where it comes from and anyway she's already in, pulling the guitar in after her.

She doesn't wait for him to follow, doesn't ask him, she just goes and he is drawn in after her.

They both remain crouched on the other side of the doorway, and a short corridor stretches out before them. Nikolai remembers it vaguely from the few times he's been and knows there's an entrance farther up on the right that leads into the main games hall. It's from this doorway that the place's only light source emanates a gritty, dirty glow.

They listen; silence.

Katja stands, walks toward the light source, her hands on the body of the guitar as if it is a pistol in a holster. Peeks her head around the corner.

Nikolai only realizes he's been holding his breath when he feels his chest tighten and the sudden need to exhale overcomes him. He breathes out hard but slowly just as Katja steps inside the games hall, and he's ready for the gunshot or the shout or something, something to bring this all crashing down around them.

There is an electronic click and beep from one of the machines.

Nikolai steps inside a few paces behind her and there's the smell of hot circuit boards, the dull glitter of a few machines still running, their reflections scattered across the ceiling.

The cabinets are great dark bulks, blocky shadows like skyscrapers during a blackout, like sentries on duty.

As he watches Katja walk amongst them, he feels certain one will pounce on her, push her to the ground and crush her.

He wants her to slow down, slow down, but she won't, ducks around the final machine in the row and stops.

"Uh oh."

Nikolai swallows.

Uh oh? What uh oh?

The initial discomfort he felt at carrying a gun is now gone and he finds himself wishing for it back. Somewhere a timer clicks, clicks, clicks and it's counting down, counting down to when they are . . .

"Have a look," she says.

And it's around the corner, behind a large cabinet with a fake rifle resting on a pair of pegs.

A pair of pegs, then a pair of legs, sprawled out on the floor beneath them and from the legs a torso and from the torso a pool of blood.

Blood.

Blood.

Katja reaches out with the head of the guitar, thinks better of it, pokes the body with the toe of her boot instead.

Nothing.

There's something akin to an asteroid impact in the body's chest, a black, charred hole that exposes little pieces of his insides. They can see the pattern of the carpet he lies on through the hole.

"I think he's pissed himself," she announces as she carefully crouches beside the corpse. "Can you smell that?"

The eyes are cold and dead and they are Szerynski's eyes in Szerynski's body. Szerynski's corpse.

"This is Szerynski?"

And Nikolai realizes that he has been talking out loud.

Nods.

"Was Szerynski," Katja corrects herself.

She looks for a moment as if she is going to touch the wound but thinks better of it, and Nikolai finds himself going from that gaping hole to the hole in her neck.

"Oh no. No no no no no!" Katja says.

"What's—?"

"No!"

And she drops to her knees and leans down toward the shadow of blood that seeps toward her, and there is something glittering there. She grabs something and holds it up.

"No!"

A piece of glass. Thin. Rounded.

And Nikolai sees, as she turns it slightly toward the glow of one of the cabinets, a fragment of watermark.

"NO!" And she throws the piece across the room, a shooting star of light that vanishes into the darkness at the rear, shatters into something out of sight.

"Fucking hell!"

She jumps to her feet, swings the guitar around and smashes it into one of the cabinets' screen again and again, frantically, desperately, and she doesn't hear Nikolai tell her, "Wait" until he touches her on the hip and she swings for him instinctively and the instrument whistles past his forehead.

"Stop!"

In his hand, another piece of the shattered vial, this the curved bottom of the piece with a splinter of glass like a half-inch blade up one side. There's a tiny amount of liquid left in the bottom. He offers it to her and she sniffs.

"Smells like piss," she says. Her trach tube quivers in her throat at the exertion of smashing up the cabinet.

"I think it *is* piss."

"I don't . . ."

"A fake," he says.

Katja stares at the pieces, sniffs again. "Just because it smells like piss, doesn't mean it's a fake."

"I've heard that's what they do," Nikolai lies to her. "As a safeguard to people trying to steal chemicals. Use fakes filled with urine."

For a moment he isn't sure if she's buying it or not, if she's trying to figure out why he's so certain it's a fake— what else he might know. Then Nikolai says:

"Maybe that's why he was shot."

"He was trying to screw Kohl over?"

Nikolai shrugs. "Something like that."

"But I saw Aleksakhina bring the vial in here."

"So maybe Szerynski *did* have the real vial."

"Then where did this one come from?"

Click.

132

Katja says, "Kohl brought it."

"And if the fake is here . . ."

"Then Kohl has the real one."

"An exchange?"

"Or a robbery," she says, staring down at the gun lying against another cabinet. She stoops down beside it, hesitates, then picks it up.

It's the gun Nikolai dropped outside.

Now here, next to Szerynski's corpse.

Nikolai flinches as pain shoots through his hand he realizes that he's down to the nail bed on his right forefinger. A little bead of blood works its way through the soft flesh and he begins on the next finger.

"Kohl must have the real vial," she says. "Kohl has it."

The voodoo lighting flickers as a rolling demo comes to life on one of the machines. Pixels dance on the previously blackened screen.

"You know this Kohl, then?"

Shrugs.

"Is he a dealer? Your dealer?"

Shrugs again. For some reason he feels ashamed to admit he uses at all. Wants to explain that it's not his fault. His stomach . . .

"Then you'll know where we can find him," she says.

This fucking night is never-ending.

Feeding Kohl a fake vial and Szerynski ending up with it, Szerynski who now lies dead at their feet and they'll think it's him, they'll think he's behind all this.

It's a vortex, a snake swallowing its own tail.

And then there's Katja at the centre of it, spinning wildly, dragging in everything around her, dragging Nikolai in.

He knows what comes next.

"We're going after Kohl, right?"

CHAPTER TWENTY-ONE

G *ot the stupid fucking thing in my hand now. Let's get this shit over with.*

Kohl walks into The Digital Drive-by. This time, it's an air of superiority, of satisfaction, that surrounds him rather than his usual twitchy nervousness that follows him like a small swarm of sticky flies.

He nods to some of the regulars, hunched over cocktail machines, their faces emaciated from the glow beneath them. It's good to have the regulars there often, providing a show for those who wish to be like them and a challenge to those who think they can beat them—either way the money rolls in.

And yet what is that compared to what he might now be in line for from Szerynski?

Beng, a six-and-a-half-foot Croat who had won local

championships on the last three occasions, nods to Kohl as he walks past, his hands continuing to move deftly over the joystick and keys without his full attention. Kohl thinks perhaps he'll organize a lock-down tournament, shutting out the small timers and amping it out to get some big money going. Why the hell not? Things were going well.

This is his kingdom, these are his people. He doesn't need endless ego-stroking domains scattered across the island, as Szerynski and some others favour. This he knows, this he controls. He will consolidate his place, nothing more.

He pushes through a crowd and the electronic garble is broken by the sound of Fat Rita's gritty shouts. The headset she wears, it looks like a piece of her gum that's snapped around her head and over her ear. Her chubby hands defy reason as she sorts through piles of coins with the skill of a surgeon.

She stops talking when she sees Kohl approach.

Into the phone she says, "Oh . . . wait. Waitaminute. Here he comes."

Clamps one chubby hand over the bud-like mouthpiece.

"Phone call for you. You wanna take this?"

Her mouth opens unnecessarily wide when she speaks, enough that Kohl can clearly see the pink wetness of her tongue and the ridges of the roof of her mouth.

"Who?"

She looks down at a scrap of paper on the desk before her.

"Shariski . . ."

And the room fades away, melts like wax from a candle.

"Szerynski," Kohl says.

Fat Rita pops her bubble through the protestation. "Yah. That's what I said."

He makes a mental note to get rid of the woman if he ever finds a way to crowbar her from the booth. Motions for her to hand him the headset, and he is certain that beneath the white noise of the arcade there is a definite sucking sound like that of a leech being wrenched from its feeding place.

The device glistens, and Kohl takes it only after sliding his sleeve over one hand and wiping the metal and plastic parts clean with his other sleeved hand. The jacket will have to go now, of course. He'll burn it later.

He pulls the headset on.

"Mr. Szerynski."

Trying to sound calm, in control. No problem.

The voice on the other end says, "Vladimir."

"I'm glad you called," Kohl tells him, reaches into his pocket and takes out the vial. Still there, still there.

"Oh, yes?" Szerynski replies. "Why's that?"

"Because I have your vial. Right here in my hands."

There's a pause, a beat. "Really."

"No problems, Mr. Szerynski. No problems at all."

The electronic music, the game themes, the cheers of the crowd and smell of hot circuit boards, reflected pixels rolling across his goggles. Life is good.

"Then why don't you come right over, Vladimir. I'm eager to see you."

"Yes, sir," he says into the headset, nodding enthusiastically. "Yes, sir."

He pulls the headset off and gives it back to Rita, not even noticing that for a brief moment her fingers touch his and possibly transfer a small amount of streptococcus.

CHAPTER TWENTY-TWO

Kohl gets the cab to drop him off a few blocks from Czechmate just to be safe, even though the sky is beginning to open. The driver, an African woman with a bulbous afro and dazzling white eyes and teeth, watches him in the rearview mirror as he leaves.

Twelve steps, then a pause, two back. Another twelve steps.

He's counting in his head, making sure not to hit thirteen. Never know what that thirteenth step might hold. Broke his ankle once on the thirteenth step—though he wasn't counting that time and didn't know for a fact that it was his thirteenth step, but chances are good that it was. It had just felt like a thirteenth step.

So whenever he's out of the comfort of the arcade, it's twelve steps forward and two back (not just one, one might not be enough, he could have miscounted so two, two steps) and then starting from zero again.

He almost loses count when the sound of tires screeching across the wet tarmac comes from somewhere nearby and he freezes. Two blocks west, a battered old car careens around a corner, dark but splattered with lighter patches as if it's been vandalized, and for a moment Kohl is ready for it to drive past him and fill him with bullets, but it keeps going west, toward the heart of the city.

Joy riders or junkies, who gives a fuck.

He begins counting again, and he's wrapped the vial in tissues, got it in his breast pocket because if he does fall it's probably the safest place for the thing to be. He counts his way through an alley whose drains have started to choke on the rainwater and are vomiting their contents onto the street. He slows as he approaches another car, this one tucked up behind a dumpster, looking for signs of occupation, but it seems to be abandoned. As he gets nearer, he realizes the tires are all flat and he relaxes slightly as he passes it.

Ten. Eleven. Twelve.

Stop. Back one. Back two.

One. Two. Three . . .

He leaves the alley, can now see the arcade across the junction. The place is deserted, too quiet to be comfortable in, but he keeps going and as he gets nearer he sees that the shutters are down.

He stops dead in the street.

Swallows.

There are a dozen streets, alleys and passageways, all of which could conceal . . . could conceal what?

Ignore it.

Counting again: one, two, three, four, five, six . . .

Stops.

There's a gun lying at his feet.

A shiver of panic runs through him and for a brief moment he has to suppress the desire to turn and flee, but he remains rooted to the spot. He bends down slowly, thinking this could be yet another trap. Pokes the weapon with a fingertip. Picks it up, releases the cartridge and sees that there's still bullets in it.

A sign from whatever gods there might be? Or a warning?

He opens a small compartment at the base of his jacket, a secure pouch he built into the garment to enable him to quickly and securely hide chemicals if he was caught short.

Then one, two, three, four, five, six . . .

Stops at the corrugated metal entrance on the twelfth step. Stretches for the buzzer but can't quite reach. Just one more step.

But no.

Two back.

Then three forward.

One.

Two.

Three.

Presses the buzzer.

Several moments pass, then there's a shrieking and

Kohl's heart rate suddenly triples before he realizes it's the shutters and they're slowly being raised.

Booted feet and heavy trousers and a shining belt buckle and Szerynski, Szerynski, Szerynski.

"Vladimir."

The man rolls his arm to invite Kohl inside.

A single light leads them into the main games room and Kohl is distinctly aware of the shutters automatically closing behind him again.

He considers that perhaps he should have brought someone along with him, Misha or one of the others, but it's too late now.

"Sit," Szerynski commands, motioning toward the only lit booth.

Kohl sits, uneasy in the brooding, oppressive atmosphere the dead machines create. He would always retire to his room on the top level of The Digital Drive-by before the machines were shut down. It always felt to him as if an execution squad were at work as the plugs were pulled and the screens went blank.

There is a ticking somewhere.

"I'm glad you came, Vladimir."

Kohl nods, unsure of what other response to give. His hand lingers over his breast pocket, fingers twitching.

Szerynski's eyebrow arches. He holds out one hand, palm up.

Kohl reaches inside his pocket, pulls out the vial, lost in amongst a mass of sodden tissue. He unravels the clotted mess onto the tabletop then holds out the vial, hovers it above Szerynski's hand.

He sees the fat lines of chemical scarring that reaches up to the webbing between the man's thumb and forefinger, crosses over toward his knuckle.

The vial drops.

Szerynski flicks it with two fingers, twists it into an upright position.

"This is the vial?" he asks, and at first Kohl doesn't realize it's a question.

"Yes, Mr. Szerynski."

"You got it from the mule like I asked you to?"

Slowly this time. "Yes, Mr. Szerynski."

The chem lord has a small torchlight in his hand now, flashes it across the surface of the glass.

Then he presses down on the rubber cap that seals the container, squeezes it out.

Sniffs, replaces the stopper.

"You see this, Vladimir?"

And he tilts the vial toward Kohl, the torch still shining upon it.

"The watermark?"

"Closer."

And Kohl can see a row of tiny numbers glittering on the inner surface of the glass.

"It's a tracking code," Szerynski explains. "We use it while we're developing chemicals, transporting them from one place to another, but particularly when they're heading to or from the mainland. Dracyev uses them too."

Kohl, he feels his eyes starting to dry out, knows he

should have taken his drops before he left but in the eagerness to get to Szerynski . . .

"The person who told me about the vial also fed me the tracking code."

Kohl reads the numbers aloud in his head.

Zero. One. Three. One. Six. Two. Zero.

"The code he gave me, Vladimir, is zero-seven-nine-five-zero . . ."

Eight. One. One. Zero.

". . . seven-zero-eight-eight-nine-seven."

Kohl's tongue is like a dead lizard that has been shoved in his mouth.

Szerynski's light vanishes from the vial and Kohl finds himself following it uncontrollably—to a second vial held in the man's other hand.

"This was delivered to me earlier this evening," he explains. "Do you see the code, like the one on your vial?"

"I . . ."

"Read it."

Kohl's gripping the table now.

"Read it."

His eyes are burning; he can't focus for several moments.

"Zero. Seven. Nine . . ."

Pauses, glances at Szerynski whose expression betrays nothing. "Go on."

"Five zero seven zero eight eight nine seven," Kohl finishes quickly.

Two vials, one in each of Szerynski's hands.

"You see the problem we have. Don't you?"

Kohl licks away a bead of sweat that has gathered on his upper lip.

What has that little fucking addict done to me?

"I can explain."

"Of course," Szerynski says genially.

"Something came up, Mr. Szerynski, something very important. I had to attend to it but . . . but you had asked me personally to do this, this, this thing for you and I had every intention of getting you the vial."

"Which you just a few minutes ago told me was exactly what you did."

"Yes. And I did get it."

"From the mule."

A beat. "Yes."

"You got this vial from the man that I sent you to? This is what he had?"

"I . . . believe so."

"You believe so?"

"Mr. Szerynski, you asked me to get the vial for you and I was going to, I had every intention of doing so but something came up, something important, and I had to attend to it, you see, and so I had to . . . delegate."

This last word spoken like a doctor would announce a terminal disease.

"Delegate," Szerynski repeats flatly.

"One of my men, a good man, I trust him implicitly, you see, I gave him the address, the address you gave me, and I told him to go, to go and do the thing that you asked of me, to get the vial, the vial. I gave him the address and I told him what I wanted him to get for me, for you, for me. And that is what he brought me."

"I see." Szerynski rolls the two vials around and around in his hands. "He brought you it, you say."

Kohl doesn't understand the inflection at first.

"Your man, your trusted, *devoted* man."

Kohl nods.

"You see, what puzzles me, Vladimir, is that earlier this evening a contact of mine brought me this other vial. The one with the correct code on it. Which raises an interesting question—namely, what is this you have brought me?"

"Mr. Szerynski, I did as you asked, I got the vial for you, the vial that the mule had . . ."

Szerynski shakes his head slowly. "Well that's not possible, is it? This is the vial that the mule had. This is the vial which I asked you to bring me, Vladimir."

"I . . ."

"So I'm asking you, Vladimir—what is this you have brought me?"

Kohl is suddenly aware of the fact that Szerynski is between the door and himself. He grinds his teeth together.

"Mr. Szerynski, please. There's obviously been some confusion somewhere. Perhaps my man, perhaps he picked up the wrong vial or . . ."

"Perhaps."

And Kohl, he's thinking, *You fucking junkie, you think you can fuck me over, you little piece of shit.*

"You think you can fuck me over, you little piece of shit?"

Szerynski, stealing Kohl's thought.

"Mr. Szerynski . . ."

A knife, he's got a fucking knife, where did that come from?

Kohl presses himself back against the booth's seating, raises both hands in a placating gesture.

"Please . . ."

"Don't beg, Vladimir. Never beg."

Eyes itching, itching. And there's nowhere to go.

Fucking Nikolai! Never should have trusted the junkie . . .

Szerynski stands suddenly and Kohl leaps to his feet at the same time, ready for what might come, hands still raised before him.

And something batters against his hip and he remembers the gun.

"The only thing worse than begging," Szerynski continues, slowly making his way around the table toward Kohl, "is betrayal."

"No . . ."

Szerynski suddenly lunges at him and Kohl rolls instinctively, the knife slashing him across his chest as he does so and he cries out, already going for the gun, stumbling away from Szerynski.

"Wait!" he shouts as he slams into the back of one of the games cabinets, bounces off it.

Szerynski stalks toward him as Kohl regains his balance, still fighting with his jacket to pull the gun out. The chemical lord holds the vial Kohl brought him in one hand, the knife in the other.

"There's nowhere to go, Vladimir," he says softly.

A short stalemate settles before Kohl suddenly dives

around behind the cabinets and Szerynski is chasing after him, charges around the corner and finds Kohl lying on the ground, hesitates for just a moment, and that gives Kohl enough time to pull out the gun, point it—and shoot.

It hits Szerynski clean in the middle of his chest, shattering the vial on its way and sending him crashing backward. Without missing a beat, Kohl clambers to his feet and charges toward his boss, fires another round at him, another.

Szerynski slumps to the ground, motionless.

By the time his final breath has dissipated amongst the pixel-dust, Kohl realizes the mess he's in.

He drops the gun reflexively, as if it will make any difference.

A little wisp of smoke emerges from Szerynski's chest.

He rushes back to the booth, finds that the other vial, the real one, is still resting on the table. He picks it up, shoves it back in his pocket. Notices blood splatters up the side of his jacket, wipes at them.

He hurries back along the corridor, then listens for a few moments through the metal shutters of the front entrance. He expects to hear the sound of Szerynski's men charging across the open lot, ready to cut Kohl to ribbons, but there's nothing.

He knows he has no choice but to go through, but he can't figure out the opening mechanism and so has to shove his hands under the small gap at the bottom and force it up until there's enough space for him to slide under.

He squeezes through and back out into the chill night air.

PART SEVEN
A NEW PLAYER

CHAPTER TWENTY-THREE

She walks through the corridors that weave their way around the main complex of labs like a mythical creature fumbling through a haunted labyrinth, but in this case it is she who haunts the place.

Her name is Ylena and this is what she does each day, every day—but only because there is little else for her to do.

She peers through a Perspex window that looks into a room in which a half dozen workers move around, connected to a thick pipe by hoses that plug into plastic casings on their backs. They wear protective masks and goggles as they work on filtering substances through an elaborate series of funnels and tubs that resemble upturned bass drums.

One of them catches her looking at them and waves. She touches her fingers to the Perspex in response, almost longingly reaching out to him until he returns to his work.

More nods and smiles as she walks farther down the corridor, and she can feel them watching her once she has passed, perhaps studying the sway of her hips or the curvature of her lower back where it is exposed by her dress.

She wears the dress hanging from her shoulders, exposing her back and, as she walks, her thighs and calves. She is a princess walking amidst white-coated paupers. But of course, that is what he wants her to be.

She walks past an open door out of which one technician leans, gasping for air as he waves away a cloud of noxious yellow gas. In the background, she sees two others laughing hysterically and it brings a smile to her face. It is not often she hears laughter.

She continues toward the end of the corridor, returns the greeting of a young female technician who wears glasses that make her eyes look like those of a turtle. She leans around the corner and there is a row of seats, perhaps twenty or so, of which about half are randomly occupied.

These people do not wear white coats. Their wardrobe is that of threadbare jackets and torn trousers, of tattoos and scuffed shoes, of dirt beneath their fingernails and swollen purple veins. They each hold a slip of paper containing brief details of the procedures they will be put through that day and, if they are lucky, a note on how much they will be paid in return.

Today she studies them from around the corner but there have been times when she has sat amongst them, as out of place as a bright red poppy amongst a collection of weeds. She has even held one of the slips of paper, reading the instructions as if she truly believed she would be party to them, closing her eyes and imagining herself being led into one of the rooms and being fed or injected or sprayed and perhaps dying there on the cold, tiled floors.

Her reverie is interrupted when she feels a vibration next to her thigh and her breath catches with surprise. Some of those in the chairs look up at her, a few recognizing her, and she ducks back around the corner, slaps a hand to her thigh.

Her heart is racing now and she checks the corridor both ways. There is a handful of technicians at the far end in deep conversation with one another, so she opens the door of a storage cupboard and ducks inside.

She reaches into her dress and pulls a cell phone from her garter belt.

She presses the answer key.

"It's me," a voice says.

She whispers emphatically, "I told you not to call me like this. What's happened? Is something the matter?"

And she's watching the edge of the door jamb for the splinter of light that would appear should someone find her here.

"It's too dangerous," she says. "What if he catches us? Okay. I'm just scared that . . . I miss you. I have to go . . ."

And she ends the call, finds herself out of breath from trying to remain quiet as her heart rate continued to increase. She switches the phone off completely and slides it back into place next to her thigh, pulls the dress over it.

She licks her lips, her mouth suddenly bereft of moisture, takes a deep breath.

She opens the door just a crack, listens for the sound of approaching footsteps, then opens it farther so she can see into the corridor beyond. The technicians are still at the far end, arguing now over something attached to a clipboard one of them holds.

She slips back out of the cupboard and quietly closes it behind her.

"Ylena."

She just about shrieks with fright at the word spoken so close to her that she can feel breath on the back of her neck, and she snaps around to see Dracyev standing before her. His black-gloved hands are by his side, fingers poised like that of a gunslinger. His lab coat is black too, and made from a thin plastic or rubber rather than the standard white fabric his technicians wear. His hair is gelled back from his face so the reflection of the strip lighting overhead looks like blue waves upon it. His beard is pencil thin and razor sharp, framing his angular face and wide jaw.

"Here you are," he says.

And her heart is racing again; it feels like the time he injected her with an amphetamine he'd developed called ZR-69. He'd taken a dose himself and they had fucked for most of the night while riding its chemical tide.

"I've been looking for you."

"I needed to stretch my legs," she says. "I was getting claustrophobic locked up in that room."

His eyes go to the half-closed door behind her.

"I felt sick," she tells him. "I thought it was a bathroom."

"You were sick?"

"No."

"Perhaps you've caught a bug or something. An infection."

"Perhaps."

He places a hand on her shoulder, runs it along until he reaches her neck, slides his gloved fingers around her.

"You should go back to your room. Rest. Then you'll feel better."

"Yes," she says. She feels the tension in her muscles and tries to force them to relax, willing them to soften.

"Besides, I have a surprise for you—later tonight. I want you to be ready for it."

"A surprise?"

He smiles and his fingers leave her shoulder and slide down her chest. "Go rest for now. I'll send someone for you later."

Ylena nods, lets him lean in to kiss her and she tastes the chemicals in his mouth. His tongue is dusted with them and now so is hers.

CHAPTER TWENTY-FOUR

He knows something has happened before the arcade's shutters have finished their crunching descent, before he reaches the car and sees that one of the rear doors is open. Before he sees that Katja is gone.

His jaw flexes in anger and he drops onto the vehicle's hood the bag Szerynski has given him, hears a noise coming from one of the nearby alleys.

"Katja!" he shouts, striding toward the dark passageway. The sound of footsteps echoes toward him and he instinctively reaches for his gun. He is not in the habit of drawing it and certainly not for someone such as Katja, but he knows how desperate people can become and he knows what people are capable of when they are desperate.

He knows this intimately.

He shouts again, sees a flash of movement and again,

entirely on instinct, shoots. The shot hits something solid and metal and ricochets once, twice. He takes another step into the alley, prepares to fire again . . . then lets the weapon drop.

Fuck it.

What did it matter anymore? Let her run. Let her be free. He is tired of locking people away.

He takes the bag from the hood and shoves it into the passenger seat, climbs into the car. He kicks it into reverse, stops as he comes level with the alley and has one last look, and is relieved when there is no sign of her. He briefly wonders how the hell she managed to get out but kills the thought. No longer matters.

The vehicle's tires screech wildly as he drives back out onto the wet streets and he can't help constantly looking down at the bag on the seat beside him.

He pulls up outside his apartment a short time later, kills the engine and sits there for a few moments. His breath steams on the cold glass of the windscreen, distorting his view of the apartment beyond. His fingers are clamped around the steering wheel.

Now the bag beside him is a lump of guilt. He picks it up, takes it into the apartment with him.

It is cold and dark inside, smells of damp.

He switches on lights as he goes.

Climbs the stairs and the damp scents are replaced by sharp, aggressively medicinal ones. He moves gently across the landing, stops before the bedroom door.

Listens.

Then opens the door, quietly, leans in.

And she is there on the bed as she always is.

Her eyes flutter, his bony chest rises and sinks and he knows she is in a deep, chemical-assisted sleep. There is a chair beside the bed, the book he had been reading the previous night still perched open on the seat. He lifts the book out of the way, sits down.

He takes the pill bottle she clasps in her hands and places it next to the rest of them, scattered across her bedside table like the fallen troops of an ambushed army. The bottles are of differing shapes and sizes but most are stickered with the same faded labels, the ones Aleksakhina himself made using the old typewriter in his office, copying the names from a medical encyclopedia, inventing dosages for her. Filling them with cough drops or powdered candies from the corner store, or the fakes the drug teams sometimes used on sting operations.

The only real ones are the sedatives she needs to get to sleep.

He touches her pale wrists, feels like he should squeeze some of his own warmth into her but can't bring himself to do so. He is as fake as the placebos when around her.

He sits with her, watching her breathe, for how long he does not know, then opens up the bag. It is stuffed with ugly banknotes that seem to have soaked up the electronic glitter of Szerynski's arcade, now sparkling as he lifts a small handful out.

He places them upon his wife's chest, then spontaneously adds a few more.

Guilt again.

He leans over, kisses her on the forehead. Her softly puckered skin retains the impression of his lips for a few moments as if it knows that this will be its final contact with him.

He wants to say sorry, feels that he should, but again the sentiment refuses to come. He closes the door behind him, goes back down the stairs, stops by the phone.

He begins to dial without thinking and hangs up just in time, one digit away from the complete number. Would it matter if his calls were traced now? Perhaps not to him but he'd already done enough to his wife. If someone came looking . . .

So he leaves the apartment, trying to persuade himself that this is just another normal night, that he is merely leaving to begin another shift, so that he can make it back to the car without having to fight with himself the whole way.

And then he thinks of Ylena and his pace quickens, past the car and to the payphone on the street opposite. He inserts the last few coins he has and redials the number he first tried in the apartment, completing it this time.

The call is answered almost immediately and at first there is silence.

Aleksakhina is hesitant, wondering if perhaps there is someone else on the other end of the line, just waiting for him to speak.

Finally a low, husky voice says, "Hello."

"Ylena." The word bursts from him with relief. "I must see you. I have the answer . . ."

CHAPTER TWENTY-FIVE

After being caught out that afternoon, Ylena placed the phone under the pillow of the bed she now lies on. She turned the phone back on not long after returning to her quarters but switched the ringer off because she saw the shadows of Dracyev's men beneath the gap in her door.

She lies back and stares at the fabric above her, a large square of intricately patterned cloth that hangs from her four bed posts. She follows the curvature of the design around and around and it spirals toward a crystalline form in the centre. Then she jumps when she feels the vibration beneath her head.

She flips onto her side, grabs the phone and hits the answer button but hesitates for several moments. Her attention is fixed on the door, just waiting for someone to burst in but nobody comes.

"Hello?" Her voice low, whispered. She wonders if he thinks this is her true voice because it seems every time they speak she has to whisper.

"The answer? What do you mean?"

She's sitting up now, still fixated on the door. "Off the island? Don't be stupid, that's not possible. Look, I can't talk right now. He's suspicious. When you called earlier, he almost caught me. It's too risky, he might . . . What do you mean? Money, what money? Of course it matters . . ."

Her eyes drift from the door; there's a tingling in her spine.

"I . . ."

A shadow flashes across the floor and she almost drops the phone, but it is fleeting and she hears footsteps receding along the hall.

"Tonight? But . . . yes, of course . . ."

It's all happening so fast, she feels blood shuttling through her veins, setting little fires in her nerve endings as it goes, and a smile unexpectedly breaks on her face and she finds herself saying, "Yes, okay . . . yes . . ."

She listens as further instructions are passed to her, nods in time with them.

"Okay. Midnight. No, I can be there. It's too risky for you to come anywhere near here. Yes, I'm sure. Okay."

And she's just about to hang up the phone when something else is said and her smile widens.

"I love you too," she says.

CHAPTER TWENTY-SIX

Kohl is fighting the desire, the need, to count his steps, and at the same time indulging himself in it because it is the only thing stopping him going insane with panic at what he has just done and what it might mean.

Szerynski, dead on the floor of his arcade, Kohl's fingerprints all over the murder weapon, not good, not good.

He loses count, damn it, has to stop where he is, halfway across the open streets where anybody can see him. Thinks he hears a noise coming from the arcade, Szerynski back from the dead to exact his revenge, one of his bodyguards, but can't see anybody. Movement at the side of the building?

Move.

He starts counting again—one, two, three, four, five— making his strides as large as he can, and he's almost back into the alleyway, hits twelve, takes two steps back, starts at one again, onward, onward.

Everything has fallen apart, everything will end now. There is no way off the island for him, no chance that he will be able to get away with killing Szerynski. So, what, spend the rest of his life being chased around an island no more than twelve miles long and eight miles wide? Everyone knew everyone and everyone knew him.

He is a dead man.

But he has the vial, the real vial this time, not the phony one fed to him by that fucking junkie Nikolai, the *real* vial, and he realizes it is his only way out of the whole mess.

The mule was to board a ship at the docks at midnight to take it to the mainland but would they know exactly who to expect? Would Dracyev think the transport of the vial important enough to warrant using one of his more trusted men? That wasn't really the way of the chemical dealers— they tended to rely on desperation and hopelessness in their people to ensure compliance.

And what other choice does he have?

If he reaches the boat and they know he isn't the real mule, they'd kill him for sure, if he's lucky, but then wasn't that the fate that awaited him anyway? At least this way he's giving himself a chance.

What if they didn't know who to expect, just that a smuggler would be arriving with a vial to take to the mainland for Dracyev? If he could just make it to the mainland, he would be out of the reach of Szerynski's revenge, whatever hideous form that might take.

He has to do it, knows this is his only option.

But the gun, he left the gun. What chance will he have if he is unarmed?

He checks his watch, sees that he has enough time to go back to his own arcade first before heading to the docks. But then if Szerynski's men are already looking for him, surely that will be the first place they will go. There's a gun in his arcade, hidden behind a loose panel next to his bed. But he can't bring himself to go back into Czechmate, even knowing the gun is still there.

Eleven. Twelve. Two steps back. One. Two.

He is only five or six blocks away.

He rubs his hands and only then realizes, with horror, that there are blood splatters on them. Szerynski's blood— and whatever bacteria might lie within it.

Hadn't even noticed. He wipes them on his jacket but the blood will already be working its way into his own body, invading him, penetrating him.

He has to wash his hands, get that filth off them. Get his soap. Get clean.

And get his gun.

If Szerynski's men are waiting for him, he'll be left with no choice but to run and take his chances unarmed—he might even be able to bargain his way out with the vial if it comes to it.

Hurry, hurry.

The counts are running into one another now, tripping over each other and he almost loses his balance as he reaches the twelfth step, has to wave his arms to catch himself and just about plants his foot for the thirteenth step, manages to catch it.

Two. Slow. Steps. Back.

Takes a deep breath.

Heads for The Digital Drive-by.

CHAPTER TWENTY-SEVEN

He had discarded his jacket in amongst a pile of trash a few streets earlier and kept his head down as he approached the arcade. He'd stuffed his protective goggles into one pocket, having to squeeze his eyes almost shut to keep out the light, feeling it burning through him even just from reflections in puddles beneath his feet.

The glare from The Digital Drive-by increases the pain tenfold but he forces himself to glance up every now and again for signs of those who might be waiting for him. And he realizes then that almost everyone in the place seems shifty, like they've got something to hide.

He crosses the entrance, notices Misha leaning over one of the booths, her oiled musculature glittering like a string of neon lights as the hand of a long-haired, unreasonably skinny man runs across her thighs. Walks past her, past

Fat Rita shouting at a customer, splattering the remains of a half-finished snack onto the glass separating them. Straight toward the back door that leads up to the private area, all the time expecting a hand to grab him, pull him to the floor and stab him through the—

A hand grabs him, spins him around, the sudden glare of lights squeezing his eyeballs, wrapping them in sandpaper, and he puts up his hands defensively.

"Whoah!" a voice says, and the blurry shape before him shifts. "Mr. Kohl, is that you? You okay?"

He recognizes the voice, it's Lucius, one of the regulars. Not half as good as he likes to think he is but a steady supply of income nonetheless. Kohl pushes his way past the man, hears him say something else but the words are lost amidst the electronic glitter and the fast-swelling pulse in Kohl's skull. It feels as if his brain is being over-inflated with neon garble and piercing lights.

He presses through the last of the crowds, reaching for the door handle with one hand and his goggles with the other, slipping the glasses on as he shuts the door behind him and slumps against it. Everything dies away again.

He fights for breath, squeezing his temples until the pounding begins to subside, glad for the relative darkness of the stairwell and corridor. It takes him several moments before he can begin the ascent, momentarily forgetting about the possibility of Szerynski's men waiting for him, and he's all too aware that he has no weapon, that the gun is lying on the floor of Czechmate. The gun with his prints and Szerynski's blood.

Szerynski's blood.

He looks at his hands again, his vision repairing itself enough for him to see the dirty smears across his palms and wrist.

Disgusting.

He climbs the stairs, peering over the landing above as he ascends, ready for the sight of one of Szerynski's men, ready to turn and flee—soap and gun or not.

Everything seems okay. Quiet. Too quiet?

His mouth is parched—dehydration, which isn't helping his headache any. He goes to the final door and cautiously enters his private bedroom. He flicks the light on, instantly banishing the shadows lurking in each corner, and there is another surge of adrenalin as he prepares for an attack.

Nobody there, so he rushes to the doorway at the rear that leads into his bathroom. He pops the cabinet over the sink with his elbow and it swings open to reveal a stack of fresh soap, knocks a couple of bars out into the sink and starts the water running. He shoves his hands under it and tears off the plastic coating of the soap, using both bars at once, soaping the bloodstains and bacteria, watching the water go from red to pink to clear, and he's feeling better already. The panic at being caught is subsiding, the rhythmic movements of the soap across his hands, the knowledge that it is making things better, cleansing him . . .

He shuts off the water, takes his medication bottle from the cabinet, hesitates.

Grabs another couple of bars of soap and puts them in his pocket, then goes to the loose board next to his bed, retrieves the gun. He takes a jacket from a peg on the wall, a long, heavy affair with a pimpish fur lining and a variety of pockets. And, just to be sure, he pulls a beanie on over his head, and it's as he is pulling this on that he hears a noise farther down the corridor.

He squeezes the gun in his hand.

A floorboard creaks and then he hears voices.

They're right outside.

CHAPTER TWENTY-EIGHT

A floorboard creaks and she hears voices.

They're right outside.

Is this what he calls love? Ylena thinks. This love he professes, this protection with which he mummifies her?

She has already changed out of the dress and into a pair of tight latex trousers and a black crop top she can cover easily with the flowing purple fur-lined overcoat she wears over them. She sits at her dressing table, combs her bleach-blonde hair back and pins it up with a set of Chinese needles, applies dark red lipstick and bruises herself with kohl. Splashes herself with perfume.

She looks at her reflection and wonders: *Is this the face of a liar?*

Of course not.

She opens the door to her room and steps outside. The

SIMON LOGAN

corridor is lined with half-moon lights that splinter the illumination upward across the blood-red walls, all the way to the man standing at the end.

Without pausing, she closes the door behind her and walks confidently toward him; he stiffens when he notices her approaching. She smiles gracefully.

"Good evening," she says to the man.

"Miss."

"I'm wondering, have you seen Mr. Dracyev? He's late. He was meant to come for me twenty minutes ago. He told me to wait but . . ."

"Come for you? I . . ."

"He is going to take me for a late-night stroll," she says, easing her way past him with each step. "I tell him he needs to breathe more fresh air but he is busy, always busy, you know?"

And she's right next to him, close enough to feel his breath, as she says, "A woman needs attention from time to time."

And she sweeps past him, continues talking as she backs away toward the doorway that leads down into the lab complex, and he's coming after her but only half-heartedly, entranced slightly by the intoxicating sway of her hips.

"I'll go see if I can drag him away from his microscope for just an hour. Will you wait here in case I miss him?"

"Miss Ylena . . ."

"I'll be as quick as I can. If I can't find him in ten minutes, I'll be straight back here." She hovers by the first step, leg extending through the coat. "Wait for me?"

A bead of sweat glistens on his upper lip. "Ten minutes," he says, though she's already halfway down the stairs before he's finished the sentence, his uncertainty about letting her past muted by the comfort of their control over her.

The atmosphere changes as she descends, the air thickening with chemical spice and the drone of machinery, red walls abruptly changing to stark white. Into the lab complex.

This late at night there is still activity, but it is a dulled reflection of that which takes place during the day and early evening. She is conscious of how loudly the crack of her heeled feet reverberates through the long corridors and passageways. Out of the corner of her eye she glances into each lab as she passes their windows, praying nobody stops her.

She forces her pace to remain calm and steady despite the desire to run, pinning her overcoat around herself. These corridors are hers, these secret routes are all her own, stolen from Dracyev despite his best efforts to keep her caged in their private wing of the building. She has spent countless hours losing herself amongst them and so the route is etched into her as clearly as the patient numbers inked on those here for the experiments.

She hesitates when a small group of men leaves one of the labs, dragging the corpse of something small and stringy behind them, then jogs toward a door opposite when it is safe. She twists the security handle and is hit with a blast of cloying, warm air—the laundry.

She closes the door behind her, moves quicker now

because she knows the laundry workers' shifts only last until midday, past the trolleys full of bloodied garments and the bulky pressing machines, the bottles of detergent and bleach.

She stops before the rear wall, pulls a handle and opens the entrance to a chute. She feels beads of warm sweat rising across her skin as she stares down into the tight black hole before her. Not as big as she remembered it.

She looks around, grabs a large sheet from a pile nearby and wraps it around herself. She tries lifting herself legs-first into the chute but can't balance enough to get her second leg in, and the entrance is too high to squeeze in two legs at once. It'll have to be head-first, she realizes.

She pulls the sheet in tight around her and climbs into the chute. It is only just wide enough for her to get her shoulders through but she manages it, freezes when she hears a noise. It could be one of the machines switching its automated routine; or it could be the door to the laundry opening.

Ylena twists herself, jerks once, twice, forcing herself into the increasingly claustrophobic passageway, finally is in far enough that her weight shifts and she suddenly slides downward far faster than she would have liked, and her hands are caught at her side, trapped within the sheet, and she's diving headfirst toward the metal covering at the end of the chute and all she can do is turn her head to one side, turn it, just as she hits the plate, crashing out, out of the chute and dumped onto the cold, hard concrete outside.

And the force of hitting the ground is like someone has

fired a cannonball into her stomach, unable to focus for several moments, thinking she tastes blood in her mouth. She groans in pain as she unravels herself from the sheet, rolling across the dusty, litter-strewn ground.

She struggles to get her breath back, eventually sits up. The moon is full and bright overhead, the sparkling pain in her neck adding a few more stars to the sky.

She stands, checking herself over—merely bruised.

Across a small courtyard is the gate the laundry trucks use for access, one of the few original ones left from before Dracyev moved in his operation.

Although a padlock and chain hold the two parts of the gate together, there is almost a one-foot gap between them, easily enough for a slim ex-gymnast to squeeze through.

She touches a hand to her mouth and realizes there is blood there, must have bitten her tongue. She spits the blood out, wipes her lips.

Heads for the gate.

CHAPTER TWENTY-NINE

So it is a case of straight across town, bursts of speed, dragged along in Katja's slipstream until he has to tell her the next turn to take to get to The Digital Drive-by and Nikolai's senses are already tingling with electron buzz as they get near.

He points at a vacant lot across which people in various states of intoxication stagger around and toward the blistering splinters of neon lighting that marks the arcade.

"What if he's not there?" Nikolai asks her.

"Where the fuck else are we meant to look?" she points out. "You said this was his arcade, right?"

Nikolai nods.

"We need to get the vial back, Nikolai. Something is obviously going down here that is over our heads, but have no doubt that if it comes down to it, we'll be made scapegoats for everything."

"I know but . . ."

And she lifts the gun out of her pocket, the gun that killed Szerynski. Hides it again.

"Katja . . ."

But she's already gone, striding across the lot, stepping to one side to avoid a pair of men struggling with each other's clothes. He chases after her and grabs her as she is about to walk through the entrance.

"Wait, wait. What if he sees us?"

"What if? He doesn't know who the fuck we are, remember?"

Uh huh.

"But what if he does know?"

"How could he know?"

"I don't—! We don't know what might be going on here."

And he has to grab her again to stop her going in. She lashes out, stripping her arm away and almost striking him with the guitar again.

The look she gives him, it stuns him long enough for her to disappear into the pixel-crowds within. Nikolai chases after her, eyes everywhere, just waiting for Kohl to spot him.

It's busy inside but things are dropping off, the gamers who will have been stuffing coins all evening finally running low, the users' drug-highs wearing off and the groupies already stuffed into the booths, parting their sweat-beaded thighs for their favourite players. It's like the place's battery is just about to fail.

He pushes his way past a kid with a wild afro that he thinks he recognizes, tries to keep up with Katja, keep her in his sight, and each time he moves past another player, there's that spark of recognition and the fear that they're going to stop him.

Spots Katja up ahead, sweeping past Fat Rita's booth and her hand is over the pocket with the gun in it. She turns back the way she came, almost collides with him, the guitar dropping off her shoulders and she has to catch it.

"I don't see him," she says. "There must be somewhere else—private rooms?"

"Upstairs," Nikolai answers before his better sense might have stopped him.

"Show me."

He looks through the crowds at the door that leads up to Kohl's private area, but before he can say anything else she's already passed him, heading straight for it. He chases after her, is glad to spot Misha lurking by one of the booths and not standing in front of the door they are heading straight for. They slip past and into the darkness at the rear, and Katja, she just shoves the door open and steps through.

Nikolai stumbles in after her and slams the door shut, finally grabs her.

"Wait! What if . . . ?"

Her eyebrow arches, lip curls and the trach tube trembles in her throat.

"What if?" she responds, raising the gun.

Trying to get them both killed. She was trying to get them both killed, surely.

Actively fucking seeking it out.

She sweeps the guitar around so it sits against her spine, climbs the stairs with a trepidation Nikolai is grateful for. He keeps looking back over his shoulder at the door, ready for Misha to walk through.

"Careful," he whispers.

She gives him an annoyed look and keeps going.

They reach the upper landing and are presented with a series of doors. Katja leans against the first, listens into the wood. Nikolai steps up beside her, and as he does so, presses his weight onto a floorboard that creaks in protest.

They both freeze.

Nothing.

Nikolai thinks he hears something from one of the other rooms, but when he listens again for it, only silence.

Katja grips the handle of the door, ready to turn it.

Glass smashes.

They both jump back and the gun is raised, pointed at the door, she shoots instinctively and the force of the blast kicks the door open and reveals Kohl's workshop, scattered with junk and metal gaming parts.

Dark. Empty.

More noise and it's coming from another room, one farther up the corridor.

Katja pushes past him, runs by the other doors and kicks in one near the end. Her hand is shaking as she holds the gun up, ready to fire again. Then disappears inside.

At the same moment Nikolai hears the door at the foot of the stairs being swung open and glimpses the oiled, muscled arm of Misha, he runs after Katja, ducks through the open doorway. She's at the back of the room, a bedroom, standing by a window that has been smashed open, staring out.

"We've got to go!" he shouts at her and she barely hesitates before swinging the guitar at what remains of the window, splintering the rest of the glass and frame. Outside is an iron catwalk that plunges down the side of the building, and she thinks she hears footsteps echoing in the distance.

Another gunshot, but this time it's not Katja firing, Misha in the doorway with a semi-automatic pointed straight at them and Katja is through the window, then Nikolai, closely followed by another of the bodyguard's bullets and another, another.

They stumble out onto the catwalk and it creaks with the sudden weight, the bolts that hold it in place puffing out powder dust from the soft walls they have been pounded into, charge down the steps four at a time and another shot rings out.

The catwalk doubles back on itself and Katja jumps over from one railing to another, her guitar clattering against the ironwork, almost tipping her over the edge, Nikolai tries the same but catches his foot, falls headfirst into the railings. Picks himself up just in time to see Misha, leaning out of the bedroom window, her gun trained on him.

He closes his eyes, fuck it, why bother, and then there's a cracking sound and he is thrown to one side then tumbles down a short set of steps and the catwalk is coming loose from the side of the building, tearing away just beneath the window. Misha fires but the shot ricochets off the metal work and Nikolai lets himself fall the rest of the way, finally hits the wet street below and Katja is there, grabs him, pulls him away.

Then there's a pop, a crack, and the entire metal skeleton of the catwalk peels away from the brickwork and is heading straight for Nikolai. He scrambles across the sodden concrete and it slams down just behind him, sounding like a bomb dropping, and perhaps beneath that noise is Misha shouting at them but he can't tell—he's already on his feet and away.

Chasing after Katja, yet again.

CHAPTER THIRTY

They only stop running about three blocks away from The Digital Drive-by when Katja collapses to the ground.

Nikolai drops down beside her and she spits blood out and there's blood coming from her trach tube too. Her guitar crashes to the ground and a string snaps, lashes him across the back of the hand.

Katja coughs up more blood, wipes her mouth. Her chest is heaving, her skin drained of colour.

Nikolai puts his slashed hand on her back. "Are you okay?"

She nods distractedly, looks behind them to check that nobody is coming after them. The ground beneath them is wet and stinks of gasoline.

"We should get you to a hospital," Nikolai tells her.

Katja, still clearing clotted blood from her mouth and

tube, says, "We don't stop until we find Kohl and get the vial."

"But if he isn't at The Drive-by . . ."

"He *was* in The Drive-by. He must have gone through the window."

"Then he could be anywhere by now."

"Don't be fucking stupid, where do you think he'll go? He's obviously fucked Szerynski over—he's only got one option now."

"What option? I don't . . . ?"

"Tell me, Nikolai, were you this dumb before that blow to the head?"

"I . . ."

"The docks, man. He's got the vial, he's probably in some deep shit now. His only choice is to go to the docks and get off the island. Same as us."

"Are you sure?"

"What other option do we have? Sit around here waiting for Szerynski's goons to find us and this gun? It's twenty to midnight, the boat will probably be docked there right now. We *have* to go."

"But even if we do get the vial and onto the boat, you know as well as I do that's the easy part. People smuggle themselves onto the supply ships all the time but I've heard, I've heard they almost never reach the mainland. The Policie wait for you on the other side and search the boats from top to bottom before anyone is allowed off, and if you aren't allowed to be there . . ."

"Then you're thrown into the water or, if you're lucky,

chained to the side of the boat and dragged back to the island. I know the stories, Nikolai. They're just scare stories to make sure we don't want to escape."

"But . . . what if they're not? Have you ever heard of anyone escaping successfully?"

She gets to her feet, wiping a congealing trail of blood from her chin and shirt, swinging the guitar back over her shoulder.

"What the fuck else am I going to do? When they discover Januscz's body, Aleksakhina will have me back inside quicker than I can restring this guitar, never mind what Szerynski or Dracyev's men might do. You stay here if you want to but there is no way I'm going to stick around here any longer than I have to."

"But you said you needed me. That they were expecting Januscz, that I should . . ."

"If I have to do this by myself, then fine," she says as she walks away from him. "You come if you want to, Nikolai— but if you don't, then you're on your own. And don't think that whatever they might do to us if they find us on that boat will be any worse than what will be done if Szerynski or Dracyev's men find you."

And she's off and he realizes he's spent most of the last few hours watching her storm off into the distance, an unstoppable force, like a bullet fired from a pistol.

He's tired, sore, and the fire in his stomach is building again. He's thinking of another hit, of vanishing into a chemical ocean like those who haven't made it to the mainland. But she's right, the shit will be hitting the fan and whatever trouble he was in before, it's ten times worse now.

They have to get off the island.

PART NINE
GETTING OFF THE ISLAND

CHAPTER THIRTY-ONE

Crates that measure eight feet by twelve feet, stacked atop one another at the edge of the concrete and a short drop into the black waters below. Men in baggy orange and black jumpsuits and oxygen masks rushing around, operating the cranes and winches, barking instructions into walkie-talkies and megaphones. Forklifts trundling along beneath the glare of the floodlights overhead like steel-fascist dinosaurs.

The bay glitters violently and as the rest of the island dies off, this place spills into life like a virus bursting out of host cells.

Kohl is covered in a thin layer of cooled sweat, hunched beside a portable generator, glad for the thick warmth of his coat, the feel of the gun resting against his leg.

So far there is no sign of any of Szerynski's men, but then

he might not even recognize them if they were there. There are a couple of Policie but mostly they're just chatting with the loading crews. He's watching a tall, angular man with a thick beard that lingers by the loading ramp, nodding as each crate passes and is lowered into the belly of the boat.

The vial is in Kohl's hand.

Is he the contact? Just walk up to him and give him the vial?

They'll know. They'll know.

And what if the man isn't the contact?

He'll need to sneak on board, then figure out the rest. Even if they find him, he'll have the vial to bargain his way off. Threaten them with it, just crush it between his fingers and it's gone. Pour it over the edge.

Drink it.

He walks away from the relative security of the generator, heading down, makes it as far as one of the crates waiting to be loaded and hides again.

Come on. Come on.

How long until it leaves? Not long. Not long.

He ducks around the corner but the loading ramp is the only visible way onto the boat, with two Policie officers lingering nearby and the bearded man at the top. No way past.

But there must be . . .

He walks away from the shore, along the concrete path that lines the dock so he can see farther along the boat. Looking for an anchor line, a rope, anything.

And then he sees someone amongst the crowd and his

heart jumps and he dives behind another crate before he even realizes what he's doing.

What the fuck is he doing here?

There's a mechanical noise and the crate begins to move; one of the forklift trucks has it in its grasp, and so he tries his best to walk calmly away until he gets to the next crate. Peers around the corner and it is him.

Nikolai.

The fucker is just standing there, hands in his pockets, scanning the crowd. Looking for what? Kohl?

What is that bastard really up to? He is responsible for all this, somehow. Has Kohl been set up? Are they waiting for him to board the boat, to get the vial back? Is that what's going on?

Motherfucker.

Nikolai is walking away now, stepping around the loading crews, and Kohl reaches into his pocket, feels the gun. The little bastard will not be getting away with this.

They're still loading. He has time.

He'll *make* time.

He slides along the side of the crate, slipping the gun from his pocket, momentarily ducking to one side as a jumpsuited worker walks past him, then two quick strides and he's right behind the junkie.

"Hey."

Nikolai, he turns quickly and it's like he's already been shot, the way he freezes and the colour drains from him. And he's stuck, cornered, helpless.

"Are you looking for someone, Nikolai?"

Nowhere to go. The moonlight drifts across the metal of the gun.

"Because I think it's rather fortuitous us meeting here like this, don't you?"

The stupid little fucker can't even get a word out. His eyes search for help.

"You think you can fuck me over, Nikolai?"

The gun raised. Aimed.

"You. Useless. Fucking. Junkie . . ."

CHAPTER THIRTY-TWO

Katja, out of nowhere she just grabs Nikolai and presses him up against the wall, shoves her hand into his crotch and her tongue into his mouth with such abruptness that he almost chokes. Before what she is doing really sinks in, she's already pulled back, watching the Policie officer that just walked past continue on toward the bustling activity of the docks.

Nikolai tastes the remnants of her blood in his mouth as she says, "Come on."

The area is bleached with the illumination of the floodlights but they manage to wander up toward the loading crews without being stopped or questioned. There are small handfuls of people scattered amongst the workers, some nothing more than bored insomniacs or the homeless or lonely just wanting companionship—but there are others lurking around just as Katja and Nikolai must be doing.

They see one person make a sudden dash for the docked boat but they're tripped up by one of the loading crew, and within seconds two Policie officers are on top of him, dragging him away.

There are stories of people jumping off the dock with crampon-style hooks in their hands that they try to snag onto the side of the boat; of people building coffins and drugging themselves, hoping they will awaken and find themselves on the mainland; of the things done when someone is caught.

But even for those who manage to get onto the boats, they have the knowledge that the hard part is still to come.

You might make it onto the boat, but the only way you're going to get off at the other side in one piece is if you have had a route bought for you by one of the smugglers, or if you have something to bargain with.

And right now Kohl has their something.

But these are just stories.

"I don't see him," Nikolai says. "He could already have boarded."

"Maybe. But if we get on the boat and then find out he isn't there, we're fucked."

"We're fucked anyway," Nikolai points out.

"*Less* fucked, then," she hisses back. "They're still loading, we've got time."

But there's so much activity, it's hard to keep track, like trying to count the number of birds in a flock that keeps changing direction.

"We need to split up," she says.

"No!"

"What, you don't trust me or something?"

"I just don't think it's a good idea."

"You think I'm trying to fuck you over?"

"No, of course not."

"Because if I were, I could have done it before now. I might have asked for your help but . . ."

"That wasn't what I meant. What if we split up then I can't find you again?"

"If we haven't hooked up again by the time the boat is getting ready to leave, then we should both make our own way onto it and we'll figure out the rest later. You head over that way, I'll go here."

"I don't . . ."

Gone again. Yet again. Off she goes.

He just about follows her but knows that would be a bad move and stays where he is. A small fire is now raging in his stomach and briefly, just briefly, he thinks of trying to find a dealer to kill it off.

But there's Katja. He said he'd help Katja.

So he turns, heads over to where she pointed, seeking out the distinctive bulging red goggles and wonders just what Kohl will do if Nikolai manages to find him.

He looks away every time someone meets his eye, turning back on himself just to keep away from the loading crews, and perhaps Kohl is in disguise or perhaps he's already on the boat or perhaps there's another fucking boat, or what if he has other plans for the vial? What if? What if?

"Hey."

A voice behind him and he turns, thinking Katja must have spotted him and oh-shit-look-who-it-is. Dressed in a flamboyant fur-lined coat but still with those flaming bug-eyes.

"Are you looking for someone, Nikolai?"

And he's got a gun, Kohl's got a gun and Nikolai has nothing. Katja has their gun and the guitar and he has nothing, nothing.

"Because I think it's rather fortuitous us meeting here like this, don't you? You think you can fuck me over, Nikolai?"

The gun raised. Aimed.

"You. Useless. Fucking. Junkie . . ."

he walks a few paces in the direction she had indicated then cuts in between two crates and leans back out. She watches Nikolai shuffle off into the crowds and immediately follows him.

It's not that she doesn't trust him, but if he was going to fuck her over or leave her high and dry then this would be his chance—so maybe it's a case of giving him enough rope to hang himself with, but maybe not. She stays well back, but he barely seems to be paying attention to those around him, almost bumping into workers several times and only narrowly missing the swinging blade of a forklift truck.

How the hell did he manage to survive this long without being killed?

She ducks behind a crate, sidling up alongside Nikolai and that's when she hears voices, or *a* voice. She slows, leans into the crate to hear better, but it's too noisy for her to discern words, so she pokes her head around the corner.

Nikolai is backed up against a wall, eyes wide and glazed.

She nudges out a little farther, sensing trouble, spots the gun, the hand, the arm, the arm that is Kohl's. The gun that is Kohl's. Pointed at Nikolai.

Shit.

She hears the click of the safety being dropped, and without hesitation she charges around the corner, swings the guitar and connects it fully with Kohl's soft temple, sending the man flying backward into some wire mesh fencing surrounding one of the floodlights. He hits the ground with an ugly crunch and a couple of workers have stopped what they are doing to look up at the commotion.

Katja fixes them with a cold, flat stare and they return to their work.

Nikolai is still standing there, staring at exactly the same place as he was before, waiting for reality to catch up with him.

"Hey!" Katja barks. "Give me a hand here."

She rolls Kohl's body onto its side and begins going through the pockets of his jacket, and after a few moments Nikolai snaps out of it and bends down beside her.

"I . . ."

"Just shut up and search him," she says. "What the fuck is this?"

Holds up a bar of shrink-wrapped soap, then throws it away.

"Come on . . ."

A horn sounds, signalling the boat's nearing readiness to leave the docks.

And her expression changes as she reaches into his inner pocket—pulls out the vial.

Her face breaks into a grin.

"Mother fuck, Nikolai. Mother fuck!"

Light flashes across the glass. A pool of blood is forming under Kohl's head and his goggles have been shattered by the impact.

"This is our ticket out of here," Katja says. "Now let's get on that fucking boat before anything else can go wrong."

leksakhina parks his car several blocks away, winds down the windows and leaves it unlocked to encourage its theft, as if the measures were even necessary. All he carries now is the bag and the leaden weight of the guilt of what he is doing.

That and the scribbled note of the smuggler's name and where to meet him.

He walks through a small gateway some way along the promenade that runs parallel to the bay, counts the streetlights that line the way until he reaches sixteen, then stops. There is a bench to one side and a man sitting in the bench, staring out toward the glittering lights of the mainland.

Aleksakhina touches his gun, holstered across his chest, then sits down next to the man. He puts the bag between them and joins the man in looking across to the lights. Listens as the zipper is opened and closed.

"I'll count every note once we're on board and if there's a single one missing . . ."

But Aleksakhina isn't listening any more, the words blurring beneath the sounds of the tide lapping against the concrete walls of the dock.

"Hey. Are you listening?"

"I'm listening."

"I thought you said there would be two of you?"

"She's coming. She'll be here."

"Well, she'd better hurry up. I'll be over by those loaders if she arrives."

If she arrives.

And the man stands, hooking the bag over his shoulder, walks off, leaving Aleksakhina to stare out across the water.

The crashing sound of a crate being dumped onto the boat docked up the bay breaks his reverie and he walks along the promenade toward the activity farther up. He checks his watch—fifteen minutes to midnight.

If she arrives, the man had said.

Waits.

Waits.

Waits.

The minutes drop away, the air getting colder and colder. He walks back and forth and perhaps this is all going to be a big mistake, perhaps the whole fucking thing will deteriorate into a useless mess, she's changed her mind or Dracyev knows, she was fearful he knows so maybe he does, and what would he do to her, what . . .

There she is.

195

Like a beacon, like the glowing lights of the mainland. His future.

She wears a large purple overcoat, her hair swept up to reveal the beautiful architecture of her neck. And here he is, unshaven, thick in day-old sweat and coffee stains.

He rushes over to her, and the worried look on her face drops when she sees him, her arms open, and they embrace. He hadn't realized how much he feared her not coming until the flood of relief washes over him and he finds himself unable to let her go.

When they finally part, he sees the dirt on her face, her clothes. "You made it out safely?"

She nods, smiles. "Somehow," she says. "But he'll know that I'm gone soon. He'll come after me."

"He won't find you," Aleksakhina assures her. "He won't take you back. I won't let him."

He takes her hand and leads her to the loading crane the smuggler had pointed to, and the man is leaning up against the great machine smoking a cigarette.

"So she came," he says with genuine surprise, flicks the butt of his cigarette to the ground.

He gestures for them to follow him, and he leads them to a crate reinforced with metal bands. He uses a crowbar to open up one of the sides, revealing sacks of something that smells like rotten fruit stacked against one another inside.

The odour is thick and pungent, spilling out of the crate in a sudden burst as if it were a freshly opened coffin.

"Your carriage awaits," the sailor says, and they both climb inside.

CHAPTER THIRTY-FIVE

She moves like a ghost through the corridors of his labs, but as often as she might drift through them, he knows them as intimately as he knows the curves of her body, and so he has no trouble following her at a distance. Always one corner behind, one room removed, hunting her.

The workers nod and smile at her as she passes them and he knows they are picturing her down on all fours, her sweat-clotted hair pressed into their thighs, but he is content with that. He follows her to the waiting area for those willing to act as guinea pigs for whatever experiments might be conducted that day and has watched her, on previous occasions, sit amongst them.

But this time she merely glances at them before suddenly becoming rigid, and she looks down the corridor, past the window of the lab he has concealed himself within, then ducks into a storage cupboard.

Dracyev leaves the lab, walks toward the cupboard.

". . . told you not to call me like this. What's happened? Is something the matter?"

Ylena's voice.

Dracyev's jaw flexes.

He hears the buzz of a cell phone.

"It's too dangerous," she says. "What if he catches us? Okay. I'm just scared that . . . I miss you. I have to go . . ."

Then silence.

Dracyev steps to one side and waits. Several moments pass, then the door opens a crack but facing away from him. Ylena steps out.

She closes the door.

He says, "Ylena." Soft. Firm. Accusing. Questioning. Loving.

She jumps with fright but before she can say anything he leans in toward her.

"Here you are," he says. "I've been looking for you."

"I needed to stretch my legs," she tells him. "I was getting claustrophobic locked up in that room."

His eyes go to the cupboard door behind her.

"I felt sick," she tells him. "I thought it was a bathroom."

"You were sick?"

"No."

"Perhaps you've caught a bug or something. An infection."

"Perhaps."

He places a hand on her shoulder, runs it along until he

reaches her neck, slides his gloved fingers around her.

"You should go back to your room. Rest. Then you'll feel better."

"Yes," she says.

"Besides, I have a surprise for you—later tonight. I want you to be ready for it."

"A surprise?"

He smiles and his fingers leave her shoulder and slide down her chest. "Go rest for now. I'll send someone for you later."

Ylena nods, and he leans in to kiss her, his mouth still dusted with chemicals, and he spreads them into her bloodstream as if they are a marker.

A territorial warning.

He watches her as she walks away, and she turns as she reaches the end of the corridor, glances back at him momentarily, then is gone.

Dracyev's nostrils flare and he immediately strides past the guinea pigs and into a large lab at the rear of the building. There are four technicians inside, all of whom stiffen subtly when they notice Dracyev enter. He grabs a phone from the wall and punches in a number.

"I need to speak to you. I'm in Lab 67. I'll wait for you in the courtyard."

He hangs up, storms out of the room and through a back exit that leads out into one of the few open spaces in the complex. The ground is swept over with dust and miscellaneous powders, stained with dark blotches of varying colour.

A few minutes pass, then he sees the dark, lumbering shape of one of his bodyguards splintering the sunlight.

"Ylena is to remain in her room, Takashi," he tells the man, with stubble like a felled forest covering his broad chin and jaw. "I want you to make sure your men are watching her but if she tries to get out, I want you to let her."

"Sir."

"If she leaves the room, I want you to contact me and follow her discreetly. Do you understand?"

"Sir. Is there a problem, sir?"

Dracyev shakes his head as he walks away. "No problem."

CHAPTER THIRTY-SIX

r. Dracyev?"

Sitting in the car, the window rolled down, his chemical-dipped cigarette a little red light amidst the shining black carapace of the vehicle.

"I see her, Takashi."

"Do you want me to . . . ?"

"No," Dracyev says, and flicks his cigarette out the window. "I'll deal with this."

He gets out of the car, wraps his trench coat around himself.

"You want me to wait here, sir?"

He waves a hand as he walks away. "Go back to the labs, Takashi. I'll be back later."

And toward the hustle and bustle of the workers who shift the crates and boxes and packages around the docks and onto the waiting boat. He sees Ylena's bleached hair in the near distance, hangs back to watch her.

And there he is.

Half hidden behind a group of workers but it would be him, it would be Januscz.

That fucker.

Dracyev considers just ending it all now with the gun strapped to his thigh but there's something poetic about all this, something that urges him toward the idea that this is how things were meant to happen all along. That perhaps whatever gods there might be have plans for the mule and for Ylena.

He loses sight of them both behind the workers, walks briskly toward the shore but still can't see them. It doesn't matter, though, there is only one place they would be going. Fate had already decided and it had brought Dracyev here to witness it all.

So be it.

He takes another cigarette out, lights it up, and walks calmly toward the boat.

He steps past a pair of workers trying to secure a support belt around a damaged crate and ascends the ramp without hesitation. A look of anger momentarily passes across the face of the bearded man at the top of the ramp but it quickly falls away.

"Mr. Dracyev," he stutters. "You . . . nobody said that you would be coming tonight.

"Change of plans," Dracyev tells him. "Don't worry— consider this a social visit."

The man laughs uncomfortably just as the five-minute signal sounds. He motions to the ground crews to finish up as Dracyev descends into the belly of the boat.

CHAPTER THIRTY-SEVEN

He thinks it's an animal of some kind about to launch an attack on him when he first hears the sound, but as he fights through the slurry that his consciousness has become, he realizes it is the boat's horn.

The boat.

Kohl sits up quickly, far too quickly, and it feels like his head just about detaches itself from his body and he swoons back to the ground below, only just getting his hands out in time to stop himself crashing down onto the hard concrete.

He touches the place on his head where there is a burning pain, feels that it is sticky. There's a puddle of quickly drying blood beneath him. His blood.

He looks up at the moon above, trying to sort himself out, clear and organize his thoughts, and it's only then that he realizes his goggles are gone and more pain shoots through him, through his eyeballs and into the centre of his head. He finds the shattered remains of the glasses on the ground beneath him and some fragment of memory flashes across him.

Nikolai . . .

Nikolai . . . and the vial.

He checks his pockets—once, twice, again, *no*!

The vial is gone. Stolen.

"FUCK!" he screams and delivers another wicked blast of pain to his cranium.

That fucker has fucked me over again!

And the anger is a slow-burning explosion rising in his gut.

He tries to stand but his legs are weak and shaky and they collapse beneath his weight.

The dock is almost clear now, only a few crates left. The activity has dropped off. He looks at his watch and it's only a few minutes to midnight. The boat is about to leave.

So he does all he can, crawls across the ground toward one of the few remaining crates, a pair of them side by side with a large pallet that rests underneath them both. He pulls himself into the tiny gap between them just as one of the forklift trucks shoves its blades into the pallet and begins to lift. The noise of the machine drives nails into his head but he bears down on it, focusing on the image of Nikolai's face, focusing on what he will do to the little bastard when he finds him.

The vial is his.

And this time he'll make sure Nikolai gets what he deserves.

PART TEN
CONVERGENCE

CHAPTER THIRTY-EIGHT

The whole boat rattles and creaks as it leaves the docks and Katja is certain she hears the sound of bolts and screws popping out, of parts of the bulkhead peeling away. Will this thing even make it to the mainland?

She finishes pulling off the orange loader's overalls, drags her hair back. The liberty spikes have sagged into egg-yolked splinters so she breaks them up a little more, peels the hair behind her ears.

"Needing a hand there?" she asks.

Nikolai is on his back, his legs in the air, the lower half of the overalls wrapped around him. One hand has a hold of his boot, the other seems to be trapped within the tangle of material.

Katja grabs his leg and gives it one sudden tug, drags him across the floor a few inches before the overalls pop loose. His boot comes off, clatters to the metal ground and they both freeze.

They're in a claustrophobic cell of a room next to the storage bays in the belly of the boat, the first place they had found that would allow them to change out of the overalls. They listen for the sound of someone coming, but hear only the scrapes and echoes of the crates and boxes moving against one another.

Katja opens up the box that the pair of them had dragged on board and inside, resting on a bedding of hundreds of little electrical components, is her guitar. She pulls it out and examines it.

"Couldn't you have just left that thing behind?" Nikolai asks.

"Fuck no—it's gotten us this far hasn't it?" She ran her fingers along a fracture that had emerged at the top of the neck between the third and fourth frets, grimacing.

"I still think it wasn't necessary to hit him that hard."

"Hey, we're here aren't we? We got on board."

Nikolai shrugs in agreement.

"Now we just need to find the man in red."

"The what?"

"The one who's going to do the deal with us. He's going to be wearing red, Januscz told me. Now remember, Nikolai, you are Januscz, okay?"

"Okay."

"We're together."

Nods. "Okay."

They climb a short set of steps that lead back up toward

the deck and quietly sneak out when the coast is clear.

"Is he on board? How do we find him?"

"I don't know," Katja admits.

The wind is biting cold, the upper deck mostly deserted though a few figures were silhouetted against the glow of the mainland's lights. Katja stares out toward them, smiles as she fingers the vial in her pocket. She thinks of Januscz lying in a pool of his own blood, of Kohl lying in a pool of his own blood, of Szerynski lying in a pool of his own blood. All that death and violence and yet through it all they have made it to the boat, and with the vial. They are almost there.

They walk up the side of the boat, sticking close to the doors that lead back down into the lower decks and Katja spots someone up ahead. She presses herself against a doorway, pulling Nikolai in beside her. The figure seems to be facing the other direction but the moonlight is bleaching everything; she can't tell what colour his clothes are.

The he turns and it feels like the boat really is collapsing, the decking falling away from under her and she's spiralling into the dark waters below.

"Dracyev."

The word escapes her lips, frosts in the air and dissipates.

"What?" Nikolai whispers.

"What the fuck is going on?"

She presses them both fully back into the doorway, her heart now racing.

"Shit, shit, shit."

"Katja, what is it? Did you see him?"

208

She shakes her head.

"Dracyev. Something's going on, Nikolai. I don't know, but I think this might be a trap."

"What do you mean? Dracyev the chemical dealer?"

"The one that set up the deal tonight. Januscz worked for him."

"What's he doing here?"

"That's what I fucking mean, you idiot!"

She says it louder than she intended, ducks her head back out momentarily to check that Dracyev didn't hear, but his figure, back now turned, remains where it was.

"Something, something's happening. Why would he be here? Januscz never said he would be on the boat. Why would he need Januscz to smuggle the vial if he was going to be here himse . . ."

And her words drift off as something occurs to her—what if Dracyev knows what she did to Januscz? What if he was here for her?

"We have to get off deck," she says, ducks back out again.

Dracyev is gone.

Gone.

Momentary relief, then the question—gone where?

"Katja?" Nikolai whispers.

And Dracyev is there, at the end of the block of doors, coming around the corner only ten or twelve feet away, and without hesitation Katja turns and runs and Nikolai looks around, sees the figure up ahead, takes off after her. He chases her across the deck, past two workers trying to light their cigarettes in the wind, and she is grabbing at the door handles as she passes them, each one locked and slipping from her fingers.

Nikolai glances over his shoulder, sees that Dracyev seems to be jogging after them, turns back and Katja has found an open door and she dives through and it's swinging quickly shut behind her and he grabs at it but it's already shut and there's a heavy clunk. He snatches at the handle but a lock must have engaged and it won't open.

"Katja!" he shouts at the door, bangs on it.

"It's locked itself!" comes the muffled response from the other side. "I can't fucking . . . shit! It's locked, Nikolai! You'll have to find somewhere else! Quick!"

"But . . ."

Glances again, the long-coated bulk of Dracyev coming toward him and he takes off, ducks around another gap in the doors and up along a tight passageway until he pops out on the other side of the boat. Tries one door, another, another, finally one opens and he jumps inside.

CHAPTER THIRTY-NINE

The stench of ripe fruit thick around them, they are wrapped around each other in the darkness, existing only through touch, hands upon one another.

Then light floods in and the smuggler is standing there, crowbar in hand.

"Walk around if you want, stretch your legs. But don't go far. It only takes us about half an hour to reach the mainland and if you want to get off at the other side, you need to be back here in time for the loading to commence—you do *not* want to be caught out trying to smuggle yourselves across, and don't expect me to cover for you if you are. I've already contacted one of the loaders on the mainland; he'll look out for your crate and make sure no one checks it out. It's a little choppy out there tonight, though—perhaps you'd rather stay where you are."

And there's a salacious tone to his voice that makes them pull apart guiltily. They get to their feet and climb out of the crate. Ylena brushes off her overcoat, tucks some loose strands of hair behind her ear.

"You okay? You're looking a little . . . green," the smuggler mocks.

Aleksakhina waves him away, unable to say anything because he feels if he opens his mouth his stomach contents will quickly be unloaded onto the floor beneath him. He presses a hand to his mouth, leans against one of the other crates.

The smuggler shrugs and walks off, crowbar over his shoulder, shouts a reminder to them about being back at the crate and then is gone.

"Are you okay?" Ylena asks, putting a hand on Aleksakhina's shoulder.

He nods a little too vigorously and dry heaves once, twice.

He hunches over for a few moments, then straightens up. "I'm fine," he says. "Sorry. I guess I'm just not used to it.

"It's okay. I'll be okay."

"Do you want to come up on deck, get some fresh air?"

"I don't . . . I think it might be worse out there. If I see the waves . . ."

"Anatoli, they're the same waves that we both looked out at each night from the island."

"I know," he says. "You go. I just need a minute."

"I don't want to leave you."

"You're not leaving me. I'll be right here. Go on. Go see

what's waiting for us."

And the prospect softens her face into a smile. "Really? You're sure?"

"I'm sure. Tonight, *tonight*, Ylena, we will be able to look at the waves again together—but this time we won't be trapped on that fucking island. We can go wherever we want."

She leans in and kisses him, and she leaves with him a sweet, vanilla scent.

"I'll join you soon," he tells her.

She kisses him again, then climbs the metal steps that lead up toward deck.

"Ylena?" he calls to her.

She stops, turns.

"Be careful," he says.

She blows him a final kiss. "I will."

CHAPTER FORTY

It had only been because the woman had turned and run when he had looked at her that Dracyev chased after her and the man she was with. For a brief moment he had believed that perhaps it was Ylena, that she had disguised herself, but the notion quickly passed.

He knew every part of Ylena, each muscle and groove, and the way this other woman moved was far too clumsy— she lacked Ylena's grace and the beauty of her movement. The woman vanished through a doorway, the man she was with taking a different route and slipping into a passageway farther up.

Dracyev stops where he is.

Whatever else might be going down on the boat tonight was none of his business. He has only one thing to do tonight.

One thing.

He walks back along the starboard side of the boat, stands by the rails. The boat is rocking gently as the tides moved beneath it, a lyrical rise and fall that is almost hypnotic as he stares out to sea. And then his fingers clench around the railing.

There she is.

Farther up the deck, leaning out toward the mainland's shore just as he is, her chemical-blonde hair pinned up but still unmistakable. He can smell her even from here.

He moves closer to a metal box-like housing of some kind so he is partially concealed by it, and watches her.

She seems to be alone.

So where is Januscz?

Dracyev hunches down a little more, peering around the housing as she glances briefly in his direction.

Doesn't see him.

Ylena turns, wrapping her arms around herself, the dark purple fabric of the coat he remembers making her flapping in the cold winds. She crosses the deck and goes through a door just behind her.

Dracyev runs up the deck, stops when he reaches the door.

Listens in first, hears nothing.

He turns the handle and goes inside.

The sound of the waves becomes muffled as he carefully closes the door behind him. He's standing on a small platform at the top of a set of steps that lead down into one of the ship's large storage areas, looking out over a landscape of boxes, crates, and trolleys tightly packed against one another. There's an internal heat coming from the engine through one of the nearby walls, lending the air a thick, electric quality. He looks for Ylena but can't see her, then hears voices coming from below.

Dracyev descends the steps on the balls of his feet, making as little noise as possible until he reaches the bottom. He follows the source of the voices, the heat of his fury matching that which is leaching from the engine room, but he swallows the fury—for now.

One of the voices is Ylena's, the other a man's.

Dracyev draws a gun and moves toward the voices.

They're both whispering so he can't quite make out what they're saying, leans in toward a crate to listen.

Is this how things would be played out?

All his careful planning and yet it breaks down and brings him here, now—to her.

And him.

Dracyev's nostrils flare.

He considers that perhaps he should just wait, let events unfold as they would have done had Ylena not decided to betray him further, but it seems to him that perhaps fate was delivering a decision into his hands.

The man in red. The vial. All of it was just falling by the wayside.

This was just Dracyev and his betrayer.

This would be his act.

The voices rise, become clearer, and they enrage him.

Their words are poison.

He steps out from behind the crate, gun raised casually before him and there they are.

Ylena stands next to the entrance to an open crate on one side, her shadow falling over the crouched figure of her lover.

"Stand up," Dracyev says flatly, calmly, and the two jump in shock, Ylena's expression becoming one of sheer horror. "I want you to be on your feet."

"Oh my god," says Ylena.

"It's okay," the man says as he stands, raising his hands slightly. "It's okay, Ylena."

Dracyev hesitates, momentarily stunned. "Who are you?"

The man seems uncertain of the question at first and turns to Ylena who is equally confused.

"I . . ."

Dracyev realizes his grip on the gun has loosed so adjusts it, aims it toward the stranger.

"What are you doing here? Where's Januscz?"

Again the man is puzzled by the question. "Januscz?"

"Where is he?" Dracyev asks, this time aiming it at Ylena. "Where is he, Ylena?"

"I don't understand," she says, her voice as shaky as her hands. "Please . . ."

"Don't beg," Dracyev barks. "It's not becoming of you. Who is this? Is he helping the two of you?"

She looks at the man, and it still seems like something isn't truly sinking in for them; they don't seem to realize what's going on.

"I know what you've been up to, Ylena. I know what's been going on."

"I . . . put the gun down. Please."

"Don't fucking BEG!" he screams suddenly, jerking the gun toward her, and she flinches as if he has struck her with it.

"Stop it!" the other man shouts and then jerks away as Dracyev swings the gun around toward him.

"Don't worry," Dracyev assures him. "This will all end soon. Ylena, I'll ask you again—where is Januscz?"

"I don't even know who Januscz is!" she pleads. She's clasping her hands together as if in prayer.

"Don't you fucking lie to me!" he shouts and grabs her arm, pulls her away.

The stranger goes to grab her back but he's too slow, and by the time he is ready to try again, Dracyev has the gun trained on him.

"I know he's here somewhere. Just tell me where and I can deal with him first."

"Baby, please," she says, as tears run down her cheeks. "I don't know what you're talking about!"

"You're telling me that you haven't been cheating on me? That you didn't sneak away today to come onto this boat to . . . to escape from *me*?"

Her silence is full of her guilt and they all know this. Dracyev loosens his grip on her slightly.

"Tell me where he is, Ylena. Tell me where Januscz is and you can come back. We can put this behind us."

"I don't know who the fuck you're talking about!" she

screams hysterically, and twists out of his grip. She weeps into her hands. "If you're going to fucking kill us then just fucking do it!"

"Januscz is the only one I want to kill, angel."

"I don't . . . know any . . . Januscz," she says, her words shuddering through her tears.

"Then why are you here?"

And she glances at the stranger and there's something in that look, something meaningful.

Dracyev says. "So this is the one."

And she's crying through her answer, the stranger seeming to fight the urge to go to her.

"You."

The other man swallows. He is dishevelled, his hair a mess, unshaven, his eyes bloodshot and it looks like vomit glistens on his chin.

Dracyev raises the gun. "Tell me your name?"

The man doesn't answer.

"Please," Dracyev insists. "I'd like to know the name of the man who has been fucking my wife before I kill him."

CHAPTER FORTY-ONE

Kohl finds himself counting again as he walks across the boat's deck, but is distracted as his stomach rolls in time with the undulations of the waves.

Three. Four. Five. Six.

One hand always on the rail that runs along the edge of the boat as if to anchor himself in lieu of solid ground beneath his feet. The last time he was off the island he wouldn't even have been able to reach the rail. The last time he was off the island he had been taken there by a man named Varkov, a man who had treated him as both son and drug-running protégé. This time, however, he had been let on board by one of the loading crew, a junkie who had gone straight several months earlier that he had spotted not long after regaining consciousness. The withered, jewel-eyed man had submitted to Kohl's threats, of Kohl planting a baggy of powder on the man, exposing him to his employers.

That man's presence there had been fate, surely. Kohl's escape was meant to be, despite Nikolai's best efforts to the contrary, so he had taken full advantage of it.

And soon he will be on the mainland again—but not until he has the vial.

And not until he finds Nikolai.

Nine. Ten. Eleven.

Ten.

Eleven.

Fuck.

He stops, presses his hands to his eyes, the pain behind them building, swelling. Just find Nikolai, get the vial, then get somewhere dark until he can cut the deal.

There's a sudden bang and he's certain it's a gunshot, swings around and the boat lurches and, a door opens in front of him. He's still fumbling for his gun when a woman with cocaine-white hair bursts through the door and rushes past him, and a few moments later a man chases out after her. Kohl struggles to get the gun out but by the time he has it in his hands, they've already gone and he's thrown toward the doorway as the boat lurches again.

His heart races but whatever has just gone down, it has nothing to do with him or with Nikolai and the vial.

His hand remains on the gun as he watches the two disappear into the distance, and they don't even seem to notice him, caught up in a storm of their own. The woman is chased along the deck as water sprays across the hull, and just then someone steps out from the darkness of the ship's cabins up ahead.

He sees the silhouette before it fully registers with him, crooked spikes and then the glint of something metal in the middle of it all. A lip ring. The figure emerges into the moonlight and she's younger than he first thought, something blurring her throat and something else strapped to her back.

A guitar?

Reality shifts and she's standing before him, swinging something hard and gleaming toward him, and he ducks back against the door behind him, his hands going up protectively, until he realizes that she's not moved. Still in the shadows.

And he remembers.

Remembers her there on the docks when he had the gun trained on Nikolai, before his goggles were smashed and the light burst in and then went out again just as quickly.

She's involved in all this. The little bitch might have the vial.

He leans back as the girl walks toward him. The door is still open from the blonde who burst out of it, so he eases himself through and carefully closes it in front of him. The door is fitted with a vent at just below eye level and he can see the deck and the railing through it.

He pulls the gun out and steadies his grip, ready to fire.

CHAPTER FORTY-TWO

My name is Aleksakhina. Anatoli Aleksakhina."

Dracyev's aim is concrete solid, the veins along his wrist and hand thick with blood. Gun steady and furious.

"And who *are* you, Anatoli Aleksakhina?"

"I'm nobody," he answers.

Ylena, she's struggling to stifle her tears. Her hands shake as if palsied. "Don't hurt him . . ."

"Hurt him," Dracyev repeats and the gun is like an attack dog straining on its leash. "You stink of Policie."

Aleksakhina licks his lips. He's trying to survey the area without taking his eyes from the other man and the piece of metal pointed at him. A way out. A way through. At least to get Ylena to safety.

He thinks of the gun holstered on his chest, but he knows he wouldn't be able to draw it in time.

"Come to me, Ylena," Dracyev says. "Come over here and this can all be over with much more quickly."

She shakes her head through the tears. "I don't want to. I don't want to."

Dracyev's nostrils flare and, for a moment, just a moment, his eyes leave Aleksakhina and go to her, and in that moment there's a noise from behind them and everybody reacts at once.

Dracyev swings the gun around as someone steps out from behind the crates; Aleksakhina shoves Ylena to one side and, as he reaches down for his knife, there's a gunshot and for a moment he's certain he's been hit, that he's trapped in that silent moment before the pain will explode, but then nothing comes and he charges toward Ylena, grabbing her and pulling her with him. Another shot is fired and ricochets around the room then crashes into and splinters another crate.

Ylena swallows her screams as she runs, charging up the stairs that lead back up toward the deck because it's the only exit she can see, and Aleksakhina chases after her, shouts for her to wait, although that isn't what he wants, he wants her to run as fast as she can, and he's just waiting for more shots to come their way.

She bursts out through the door and cold air washes over him as he follows her out, calls for her to wait but his words are consumed by the sound of the crashing waves. She cuts across the deck between a gap in the cabins and he sees her stumble through the tight space and crash into the railing at the opposite side of the boat. She pulls herself along the rails, her legs threatening to collapse beneath her, follows them all the way to the back of the boat, pins herself against it.

Aleksakhina reaches her moments later, and she looks as if she is going to try to duck away from him but he's too fast. She's hysterical, completely out of breath and shivering so badly she can barely stand up. He grabs her just in time but she pulls him around, looks behind them.

"He's coming!" she shouts. "He's coming!"

Aleksakhina turns, can't see Dracyev but knows he'll be there in a few moments, the gun aimed and ready once more.

"We have to hide!" he shouts to her.

"He'll find us! He'll fucking find us! Where the hell are we going to go?! There's nowhere to go!"

"Ylena, no!"

And he grabs at her as she pulls herself up onto the rails, but she kicks at him and the boat rocks, tips him away from her.

He thinks he hears another gunshot and looks back but there's still no sign of Dracyev, and when he turns back she's dragged herself up onto the tiny ledge beyond the railing and is balanced precariously on it. The boat lurches again and she has to hook a leg around the rail to stop herself being tipped off.

"Ylena!" Aleksakhina cries and grabs her hand but it slips quickly through, soaked in slippery sea water. He snatches again and gets a grip of her coat but there's not enough leverage to pull her back. "You have to get back down!"

She shrieks, a cry of pure rage and fear, and what's in her eyes doesn't even seem to be human as he tries to pull her back.

"He's going to find us!" she screams, pulls away from him. "He's never going to let me go! I should have known I'd never get away from him!"

The water kicks the boat and throws water up over the side, knocks her hair loose and the pure blonde strips lash against his face and she has become Medusa. Aleksakhina pulls at her jacket and she jerks toward him, but then his grip is suddenly lost and she pops out of his grasp and her momentum swings her backward.

She grabs at his hand but misses, is falling away from him, and he shouts her name and she desperately tries to snatch at the railing but she misses that too, then she's gone . . .

CHAPTER FORTY-THREE

The thrum of the boat's engine vibrates through her so thickly that Katja has to fight the sensation that she is drifting into the air. Her skin is coated in a thin sheen of oily sweat, enough so that it's hard for her to grip the neck of her guitar properly.

She's pulled off a broken string and some of the lacquer that was cracked when she hit Kohl, and the thing's a fucking mess but it doesn't matter, they probably wouldn't even be on the boat if it wasn't for the guitar. Eventually she makes her way back through the machinery she passed when she dived into the engine room and away for Dracyev, the sound of Nikolai banging on the door still in her ears.

She hadn't meant to leave him stranded out there, she really hadn't, and that strange feeling in her chest, could that be guilt? More likely indigestion.

There is a pair of huge bolts and latches sealing the door shut. She leans forward, can see through some slats in the door and out to the deck. No sign of Dracyev. No sign of Nikolai.

So something was definitely going down but she's come too far already; there's nothing left to do but just keep going. She still has the vial and if she can find Nikolai again and they can make the deal with the man in red, nothing else would matter. As soon as they reach the mainland, the murders, the chemicals, and whatever shit Januscz was involved in will be left behind.

Everything will be left behind.

She pulls at the locks and though they are stiff and heavy, she manages to open them both. She holds the door steady, steeling herself for going back outside and for what might be out there.

Dracyev, his gun ready for her.

Or Nikolai's body sprawled across the ground, just one more in a long line of bodies.

She's just about to open the door when she hears a muffled bang, then a few moments later what sounds like a scream. She freezes where she is, peers through the slats in time to see a woman running along the deck and then a moment later another person chasing after her.

What the fuck is going on *now*?

It's beginning to feel like all the trouble on the island has been condensed into the boat for this one night, that everything she is trying to escape from is following her to the mainland.

Another few moments and she eases herself out through the door, and the fleeing couple are gone. She stops the door from shutting properly, wanting to know that there is at least one escape route for her should she need it, then makes her way through the shadows of the cabin buildings.

Her sweat chills on her, bruises her like the result of a vicious assault.

She tries each door as she reaches it, whispering Nikolai's name through the slats but they're all locked. She thinks she hears a door closing or opening farther up but it could just be a random part of the boat rattling or squeaking.

"Nikolai?"

A horn sounds suddenly, makes her jump, and she realizes it's the signal for ten minutes to shore.

They're running out of time to find the man in red and make the drop.

Another door, "Nikolai?" and another.

Each one locked—where the fuck has he gone?

"Here."

The word takes a few seconds to register and she stops. Turns.

The door in front of her opens, just a crack.

"Nikolai?"

Her hand goes to the guitar's neck but before she's got a good grip, the door swings open and someone bursts out and shit, it's not Nikolai, it's not him, and it's too late, her arms are grabbed, something smashes her face and she staggers to one side and then the wind and the waves go silent and the sound of the door being slammed shut echoes around her and all she thinks as she crumples to the ground is, *The vial, I'm going to land on the vial . . .*

CHAPTER FORTY-FOUR

Technically, he's a serial killer now.

Nikolai, standing over the body of yet another victim, another person he's killed. He supposes that, to be pedantic, this is the first one that he has actually killed himself but it was because of him that Katja had to smash Kohl over the head so at the very least he's an accomplice.

Clyde to her Bonnie.

Sid to her Nancy.

But Januscz was dead before he even met Katja and Szerynski so that's hardly his fault either.

Yet it seems like on this night he can't go anywhere without someone dying because of him or at his hands.

And this one, this one was definitely his fault.

Dracyev, there at his feet.

There was no disputing that he shot the man. His kill.

His victim.

And there was no doubt it was Dracyev—Nikolai knew of him as well as any of the dealers.

In the matter of a few hours, he has stood over the smoking, bleeding corpses of two of the island's most powerful chemical lords—so if he hadn't needed to get to the mainland before, he certainly did now.

On some distant, numbed level of consciousness, he is aware of the sound of a door slamming shut, perhaps the same one he escaped through to avoid the man now lying dead at his feet, or perhaps the one on the opposite side of the storage area. He'd heard the voices and panicked when he saw them all standing there, hadn't even meant to pull the trigger but somehow he had.

Or maybe it had just gone off, fired itself without any input from him, the events unrolling around him as quick and uncontrollable as the debris flung around by a typhoon.

He doesn't know what it was he interrupted and doesn't particularly care, but that doesn't mean those he interrupted won't care. Add two more to the list of people out to get their revenge on him.

If Katja were here with him, what would she do?

Hide the body. And get out of there.

Yes.

He stuffs the gun into his pocket, hesitates, then takes Dracyev's weapon too, cringing as he has to pry the dead hand open. Then he pulls the body toward a crate with one of its sides partially crow-barred open and it's only partially filled with sacks and boxes of strong-smelling food, a few pieces of polystyrene, and a weight in each corner. He struggles to get the corpse inside, the growing pool of blood appearing upon Dracyev's chest making it difficult for Nikolai to get a decent grip, and several times he drops the man to the ground with an ugly, echoing thud.

Sweat is rolling from his brow as he maneuvers the body toward the back of the crate, shoving some of the sacks up against it in a vague effort at camouflage, then closes the side of the crate back up again as best he can. The nails have been bent by whomever opened it so it won't seal properly, but it'll have to do.

Now to find Katja.

He's just taken the first step onto the stairs that lead up toward the door and the outer deck when he hears the blast of the boat's horn signalling the final approach to the mainland.

Shit, have to find Katja, have to find her now or there's no fucking way I'm getting off this boat.

He charges out into the freezing winds, vaguely realizing how comfortable it feels wielding two guns now.

nd her wrist like bone china, this wrist that he has put his mouth to and dreamt of being twinned with his own, it's all that's stopping her from dropping into the vicious ocean below, waves snapping at her heeled feet like the jaws of a pack of dogs.

Her mouth is open in a scream but he can't hear her over the monstrous crash of the water and she's so white, so fucking white, against the blackness below her.

Aleksakhina manages to lean farther forward and snatches at Ylena with his free hand, but he becomes unbalanced as the boat lurches and he grabs the rail instead, and her momentum shifts, she swings away from the hull then crashes back into it, and this time he hears her, a short sharp cry of pain.

He pulls himself farther up onto the ledge, freezing

water kicked up across his face and she's just hanging there, doll-like, her cocaine-white hair having burst free of the pin she had it in, and it's like a freeze-frame explosion, like a beautiful shotgun suicide.

She's beginning to slip through his hand but he can't let go of the rail. She's sliding away from him, he shouts her name; this can't be everything they've fought for, everything they've risked, can it?

The mainland is in sight, the lights glitter for them, only for them, and he can see it in her eyes, can see how it's all going to end.

"Ylena!" he shouts at her, and he lets go of the rail, taking both his own and her body weight against his thighs, crushing them against the rail and it's all that's stopping him from tumbling over.

He snatches her wrist, drags her upward and grabs again, this time getting a hold of her other arm, and the boat lurches again and she is thrown around beneath him.

"Hold on!" he yells, and all he can think of is their secretive kisses, their stolen conversations, the thought of them spending a night together. Just one night.

All of these things they never had.

He looks around for a rope or anything he can throw to her but she's just limp in his arms, not even trying.

"Ylena, look at me!"

And she looks up at him, her eyes deep and black like bullet holes in her head, and he is jerked forward as the boat lurches again, pain shooting through his thighs and across his hips.

It's getting too much for him but there's nothing left to do but hold onto her, to be with her.

He's being moved closer and closer to the edge, his legs drawn across the rail and there's less and less to take his weight but he can't let go, he can't. He has to be with her.

That is the only way things can be.

He's pulled forward enough that it's just his kneecaps now locked against the rail but the pain has subsided or gone somewhere else, the wind, the noise, the icy winter-splatters of the ocean and he's looking into those bullet-hole eyes, their fate sparkling across them.

And the boat kicks against the ocean and his knees come loose. He is flung overboard but their hands are locked. They are pinned together as they fall, as they explode into the water.

CHAPTER FORTY-SIX

Katja tumbles to one side, thrown by the force of the blow, and crumples to her knees. Something tugs at her, sending a spike of pain up her spine but she's too dazed to react.

Her eyes hurt as she opens them and she realizes it's because a light is being shone directly at her face. She holds a hand up to shield herself but the light is still too strong.

"What a scrawny piece of shit," a voice announces.

Her guitar lies beside her, still intact but with another few broken strings, and she thinks of the vial, fumbles through her pockets.

"Whatever you think entitles you to this, you're wrong."

And the light moves away from her to the vial, held in the hand of the man before her.

Kohl.

She becomes aware of a throbbing pain down one side of her face and gingerly explores the area with her finger tips. She touches flesh before she should, swollen to high hell, and wet. She feels where the skin has broken in a neat line across a cheek as cleanly fractured as her guitar neck.

"Fair's fair," Kohl says, and once again the light's beam is redirected, this time at his bruised and bloodied face. He lets the bulb go and it swings back into place behind him, describing him in a dirty silhouette.

"So, are you fucking Nikolai or what? Did you talk him into this little scheme to fuck me over? Because I know him well enough to be sure he didn't think of all this himself."

"That depends," she answers, wiping blood from her face. "Did you plan on fucking Szerynski over yourself?"

Even amidst the shadows, she can tell his expression hardens.

"What are the pair of you up to? This is about more than the vial, isn't it?"

"This is about whatever you want it to be about," she snarls. Spits blood to the floor.

Kohl looks like he's going to say something else, stops. "Doesn't matter anyway," he tells her. "Whatever it was, you've failed. I've got the vial. I'll be cutting the deal."

"You think so?" Katja warns.

"I do," Kohl snaps, and then grabs her by a liberty spike, drags her across the floor. He smashes her once more in her broken cheekbone. He kicks open the door and pulls her across the deck to the edge of the boat, shoves her into the rail, still holding her spike, leans her over the ledge.

She fights against him as salty water sprays up toward her, and the crash of waves far below blasts through her ears, but the punch to her cheek has left her legs weak, her head glittering with nerve endings firing angrily.

Kohl presses against her, her back arching over the rail, and he's trying to grab her legs to tip her the rest of the way over but she kicks out and he can't get a hold of them both. Instead he slaps a hand over her mouth and nose, presses the forefinger of his other hand across her trach tube, shutting off the air supply.

Her eyes bulge and she's flailing, doing everything she can, but he's too strong, she rolls to one side and his hand slips and she manages to shout, "The deal won't go down if I'm not there!" But he just laughs and pushes her farther and she tips backward, onto the ledge, her legs useless, kicking at thin air.

"Januscz told them I'd be with them!"

And Kohl stops.

His grip loosens.

He pulls her back onto the deck, holding onto her T-shirt to keep her upright.

"Januscz," Kohl repeats. "How the . . . ?"

"He was going to leave me," she tells him, another trickle of blood rolling across her chin. "I made him call his contact and tell him there would be two of us, that I would be there too. That fucker wasn't going to get off the island without me."

She coughs, splutters, spits more blood, and Kohl's grip loosens further.

Two crewmen appear at the end of the deck, offering the struggling pair no more than a cursive glance and then move on, uninterested in becoming involved in trouble.

"The man in red won't let the deal go down if I'm not there," she tells him.

"What man in red?"

Katja smiles broadly, her teeth stained with blood. "You don't even know who to make the drop to, do you? Or where? What the fuck did you think you were going to do with the vial once you threw me overboard?"

Kohl's eyes are watery and bloodshot, the veins in his temples swollen and pulsing rhythmically.

"I'll know if you tell me," he says, without conviction.

"And it won't matter one little bit if I'm not there. I'm telling you, man, if I'm not with you, this deal won't go down. You let me go and we'll put this thing through together, split it fifty-fifty and go our separate ways."

"Seventy-thirty," Kohl says, again without much conviction. He's trying to figure her out, trying to judge if this is just another con or not.

"Fine, seventy-thirty, it is."

"What about Nikolai? Where is he?"

"He split," she tells him. "Couldn't handle it. He freaked out and I left him back at the docks. Useless fucking junkie."

Now Kohl smiles. He lets her go, straightens her T-shirt but remains pinned up against her and ready to grab her should she make a run for it.

"There's a man in a red suit; he's going to drop the deal," she tells him. "He's never met Januscz before—all he knows is that a mule and his girl will bring him a vial tonight and that in exchange he's to let them onto the mainland."

"You'll tell them I'm Januscz?"

"It's the only way."

"What about you? How will they know you're the girl?"

"The man, his name is Ghul," she lies, grabbing the first name that comes to mind, one of her band's many ex-drummers. "We have some history."

"What do you . . . ?"

And Katja raises an eyebrow, answering his question before he's finished asking it.

"Sure get around, don't you?"

"Luckily for you," she replies coldly.

Kohl studies her for a few moments. The boat's horn goes once more, signalling five minutes to disembark. The sounds of the loading machinery from the mainland now become clear.

"Okay," he says finally. "But if you try anything and I mean *anything*, I won't hesitate to—"

"Yeah, yeah, I know," she cuts him off, slipping out from between him and the railing. "You won't hesitate."

Kohl takes her arm and pulls her toward him. "You stay this close to me until the deal is done, you understand? This close."

"I got it," Katja complies. "Now let's get this shit over with."

CHAPTER FORTY-SEVEN

The horn sounds one final time, the boat now bathed in the bleach-glow of the mainland's loading crews stacked up against the shore in their orange-and-black jumpsuits like restless rioters ready to attack a Policie meat-wagon.

The urgent tides are pressed up against the dock as the boat squeezes into its berth, a deep grinding sound echoing through its metal body as it comes to rest. Ropes are thrown from both the boat and the dock, a symbiotic exchange as the two industrial bodies become entwined with one another.

Two trucks move forward toward loading ramps driven into place, the wheels of the vehicles mere inches from the edge of the dock. On the boat, a couple of workers secure the ramps at their end, then wave to the drivers who put the trucks into reverse. The ramps slide across the roofs of the vehicles and finally crash to the ground in front of them, nestling neatly into indentations gouged in the concrete over time.

Forklifts emerge from the warehouses looming over the scene like ancient monster-gods and manoeuvre themselves around the cranes whose motorized engines flare to life. The whole place is like a battlefield.

Amidst these rusted beasts and the drone of their machinery, a man steps out of a battered old car, a cigarillo perched between thin, dark lips. He locks the car door, adjusts the collar on the high-neck black shirt he wears, straightens his jacket. As he walks into the light, he checks the suit more fully, brushes some flecks of dirt from it.

Under the glare, the suit's red wine tone looks more like fresh blood.

CHAPTER FORTY-EIGHT

Katja, she feels her eye closing up, the fractured cheek now swelling enough to block her vision, and she's doing her best to ignore the pain in the hope that not acknowledging it will mean not being subject to its effects.

She sees the loading crews over the edge of the boat, but there're too many thoughts running through her head for her to understand that she is practically on the mainland, that she is almost there. Almost there, but still so far away. Still with Kohl between her and whatever might come next.

Where the fuck is Nikolai?

She hasn't seen him since they were split up by Dracyev; he could be anywhere. He could be watching them now, perhaps ready to make a move, and she doesn't know if that's a good thing or not. Does she want him to make a move?

She tries to look over her shoulder on the chance that she might spot him or even Dracyev, whatever the fuck he was up to, but Kohl drags her along.

A few loaders are now on the deck, opening up the hatches that lead into the storage bays, barking instructions to one another. The mighty arm of one of the cranes sweeps overhead and more floodlights are turned on. Kohl flinches away from them, tightens his grip on Katja's arm, and her instinct is to resist, to throw him off, but then she thinks of the vial and the deal and the mainland.

"Where is he? Do you see him?"

"Not yet."

"Where are we supposed to go?"

"Januscz didn't say," she tells him.

"Perfect. We're going to fucking miss him!"

"Calm down," Katja snaps, smiles as some workers look at them. "He'll be around somewhere, just be patient. We should probably just head to the loading ramps."

Kohl seems hesitant, perhaps overly suspicious of her, but doesn't let her get more than an arm's length away from him before he is next to her once more.

"You want this as much as I do," Kohl reminds her out of the corner of his mouth. "You try anything and all you'll be doing is fucking yourself over."

"I know that, you idiot."

Kohl licks his upper lip to clear beads of sweat that have formed there, too anxious to notice the insult.

"Do you see him?"

They look down the ramps, past a steady flow of

workers and out to the docks beyond. There are armed Policie officers stationed at regular intervals along the waterfront, automatic weapons slung over their Kevlar-coated shoulders.

"We can't go down there," Katja says. "We don't want to draw attention to ourselves until we've found the man in red."

"Well where the fuck *is* he?!" Kohl shouts, then immediately cringes like a dog that's just barked and knows it will get in trouble. The workers glance at them, at their bloodied faces, then move on. Then, whispered this time, "Where is he? What if we should have made the drop on the boat? What if he was on board and now he's gone?"

Katja chews her lip, looks back along the upper deck.

Goes cold.

Only six feet away, standing right there amidst the glare of the floodlights.

Kohl feels her go rigid and turns too, the lights sending spikes of pain into his eyes but he squints through it, sees the figure ahead of them.

"Is that him?" he asks.

The figure comes forward, out from the main spray of illumination. There's a patch of red on his ragged T-shirt.

"I believe you have something for me," the man says.

Kohl shields his eyes with his free hand, still holding Katja with his other.

"It's him?" Kohl asks her.

No answer.

"Hello, Katja," the man says.

"Katja?" Kohl asks, his eyes now thudding balls

burrowing into his head, blurring his senses.

And Katja, she breathes once, hard, and she's still as stiff as a board when she says, finally:

"Januscz."

CHAPTER FORTY-NINE

The guy's name is Ludomir and he's been due Januscz a favour ever since getting jumped by a psycho dealer's crew a few months back after one of Katja's gigs. Januscz had beaten them off with the business end of a mike stand, popping the eyeball of one of them before they had managed to escape.

So Ludomir, he gives Januscz the nod to be let on board the boat despite the fact he's got a gunshot wound to his shoulder that's bled out across his shirt as if it were trying to manifest the face of a god, a large curved blade clasped to his body. Januscz pulls himself into a storage cupboard filled with cleaning rags and spare uniforms, and slumps against it just as he feels the boat drifting out into the bay. His head is full of bright, sparkling air and his entire body shivers from the loss of blood and shock, but he's come all this way, he won't fail now.

He knows the bitch will be on board and this is confirmed a short time later when he has regained some of his composure and ventures out of the cupboard. He goes into what looks like one of the engine rooms and finds on the floor the battered remnants of a bass guitar. The strings are snapped, the body cracked, but he knows it's hers.

Anger flares in him.

She's here.

He picks up the guitar and turns it over in his hands, notices the blood smears, dried now—so he's obviously not the only one who's been caught up in her betrayal tonight. He still isn't sure what exactly she is up to, whether it was a spur of the moment act brought on by their argument after he'd been forced to arrange for her to accompany him, or whether there was something bigger going on. But what he did know was that she wasn't going to take his fucking vial, steal his opportunity to escape to the mainland. Dracyev had chosen him to be the mule because, he'd said, Januscz had shown himself to be a valuable asset to his organization.

He was valuable—not Katja.

And Dracyev had promised him more work, better work, once he was on the mainland—to be a part of the real operations, not just the slave base on the island. Fuck her if she thought she could take that away from him.

So he drops the guitar and quickly checks the rest of the area for any signs of her, then climbs the steps back out onto the deck again. The final signal of the boat's journey sounds and he knows this will be his opportunity. She'll have to leave the boat now and she'll be looking for the man in red to drop the deal. How she thinks she'll explain Januscz's absence he doesn't know, but then if he can find her in time he won't have to wait and find out.

He lurks behind a ventilation funnel until the boat docks, watches as the loading crews board, and just as he planned, catches sight of Katja. She's with another man, the two of them almost entwined in one another, and a new, darker anger flares within Januscz.

His grip tightens around the blade; he holds it close to his leg as he walks toward them, and they're looking for the man in red now. Januscz comes up behind them.

They have no fucking clue . . .

Katja turns and sees him but she doesn't seem to realize just yet who he is.

"I believe you have something for me," he says, loudly enough that they'll hear him over the clatter of the loading crews at work.

The man with her, his face is bloodied down one side and there are tears streaming from his eyes as he squints through them. His hand is locked onto one of Katja's arms and she's in an even worse state than he is. Her left cheek is badly swollen, split at its thickest point like a little red mouth, and a line of glistening, fresh blood trails down to her chin and trach tube. Her eye is almost lost amongst the puffy tissue, and bruises are already developing.

"It's him?" the other man asks her, shielding his eyes.

But Katja doesn't answer. Her face is stony; she swallows

and the trach tube moves in that rhythmical way it does.

"Hello, Katja," Januscz says.

That look on her face almost makes all the pain he has been in since she shot him worthwhile.

"Katja?" the other man says confusedly.

And Katja, she breathes once, hard, and she's still as stiff as a board when she says, finally:

"Januscz."

"You look surprised to see me," he says, letting the blade catch the light and flash across them both momentarily.

"I . . . I thought you were . . ."

"Dead. Yes, I could tell you were obviously concerned about me by the way you stole the vial and took off. You might at least have stayed long enough to check my pulse."

"You don't understand," she says, and her eyes motion toward her arm, where the man is holding her.

His fingers are sunk into Katja's stringy, tattooed arm. In his other hand is what looks like the vial.

"Fuck," the man with the runny eyes says. "What's going on?"

"I was about to ask the same thing," Januscz says, raises an eyebrow toward Katja.

Now both of them are waiting for her explanation.

"Listen, his name is Kohl. He works for Szerynski," she says.

"Vladimir Szerynski?"

She nods. "Or he did until he killed him this evening."

Kohl. "What the fuck? How did you . . . ? I didn't kill him!"

"He killed Szerynski, Januscz," she continues, ignoring Kohl even as he tightens his grip on her. "I saw it with my own eyes. He shot him just as he shot you."

Kohl: "What?"

Januscz: "*You* shot me, Katja."

"What? Don't be fucking stupid, I tried to stop him! Don't you remember? He broke in as we were getting ready to leave. He shot you and stole the vial, but he needed me to make the drop because the man in red was expecting both of us. He was going to force me to . . . to say that he was you, to drop the deal."

Kohl: "Shut your mouth!"

He pulls her toward him, wraps his other arm around her, one going to her neck and instinctively Januscz moves forward.

"You stay where the fuck you are," Kohl warns him. "I don't know what the fuck she's talking about. She's making all this shit up."

"Does it look like I'm making all this up?" Katja snaps back. "Look what he did to my fucking face when I tried to get away! I was trying to get back to you . . ."

"I did that because you stole my vial!" Kohl protests, looking at Januscz, not Katja.

"*My* vial," Januscz says. "And I recognize you now. You run The Digital Drive-by. You work for Szerynski."

"So . . . so fucking what?"

"So are you telling me she's lying?"

"Of course she's lying!"

Katja: "For fuck's sake, Januscz! Look at us! Does it look

like I had any choice but to come here?!"

Januscz's anger wavers, he adjusts his stance. His head is pounding, his arm ice cold and it feels like he's going to faint again. He is certain it was Katja who shot him but when he tries to retrieve the memory, there's nothing there. He remembers her catching him trying to do the deal without telling her; he remembers her forcing him to phone the man in red and let him know that she would be coming; he remembers . . . what else does he remember?

Think.

Think!

And he must have zoned out for a second because the next thing he knows Kohl is on him, the man's fingers poking into the gunshot wound and causing new blossoms of pain to explode within him. Januscz cries out and they fall to the ground, slam into the metal wall of the deck. Kohl punches him once, twice, reaches back for a third attempt, and that's when Januscz lashes out with the blade, and for a moment it's as if a pause button has been pressed because they both just linger there.

Then the blood appears on Kohl's throat; his eyes widen and so does a gap in his neck.

Januscz gives him a shove and the man topples backward, a wet gurgling noise coming from him, and suddenly there is blood everywhere. Januscz drags himself away from the body and looks up at Katja, and she looks back down at him, sprayed with Kohl's fresh blood. She turns to run at the exact same moment Januscz sees it in her eyes.

He grabs her ankle and pulls her to the ground, pulls her toward him through the growing puddle of Kohl's blood. Shocked workers jump away from the mess but they don't say anything and they keep their heads down. A few of them have heard that Dracyev was on board, which meant something big would be going down and that in turn meant they should stay well clear.

"Where the fuck do you think you're going?" he demands of her, showing her the knife.

"I . . . I thought you were going to kill me."

Januscz smiles, wipes blood from his face. "For a minute I was," he tells her. "But the man in red is expecting both of us, remember?"

He leans across and takes the vial from Kohl's hand and it too is now covered in blood, swaps it for the knife. He wipes the vial on his T-shirt, then rubs it until it gleams.

"Up," he tells her.

Katja stands slowly, watching him all the way. "He forced me here, Januscz," she says. "I swear."

Januscz rolls his tongue around his mouth, regards her as a rapist might his victim. "Later. We figure all that out later. Once we've made the drop and we're on the mainland and home free. Got it?"

She nods.

"Right now I don't know what the fuck has been going on, but I also don't much care."

She nods again.

"We just go through with as we would have done before anything happened and the rest . . . the rest comes later.

Let's just get this done."

"Okay," she says, wiping sprayed blood from her chin. "Okay."

CHAPTER FIFTY

Smoke curls from his mouth like the whisper of a recently fired gun, like the roll of a rattlesnake's tongue as it tastes the air. He wraps a hand around the boat's rails and squeezes until his knuckles turn white.

Under the glare of the floodlights, his suit is the red of infected gums.

Januscz tilts the knife so the very tip presses into Katja's shoulder blade, his other hand wrapped around her waist, easing her on toward the man in red. They walk briskly across the deck and the man in red notices them, blows out another pillow of smoke and turns away from them, leaning on the rail and looking out to the island.

The two slow as they approach him. He doesn't look at them and for several awkward moments nothing happens, then finally the man turns around.

He looks them both up and down.

Katja with blood splattered across her neck and T-shirt, congealing around her trach tube. Her liberty spikes droop and hang loosely around her shoulders, and one has dissolved completely. Her face is swollen and split, one eye now consumed by her own puffy flesh.

Januscz, his arm coated with new blood, his chest with old.

"Rough sea tonight?" the man in red enquires.

Januscz shifts back and forth, the knife blade moving against Katja's chilled skin and she tries not to react because she doesn't want to blow the deal.

"We . . . uhh . . . have the, uh . . . object," Januscz says.

The man in red's eyebrow arches. He draws on the cigar but does not exhale.

"Object?"

"The, uh, the . . ."

Januscz licks his lips, looks around nervously. Whispers, "The vial . . ."

He removes his hand from behind Katja and holds out the little glass cylinder in the palm of his hand.

The man takes it before Januscz can do anything.

"So you must be Januscz, is that correct?"

After everything, after all the deception and deals and thefts and switches and fakes and murders. After it all, here they are, as it should be, the deal about to go down and Januscz has the vial that was always intended for him.

Januscz glances at Katja, smiles, then looks back to

the man in red.

"Yes," he says, beaming. "I am Januscz."

CHAPTER FIFTY-ONE

o it has come to this.

Four years. Fourteen hundred and sixty days. Two point one million minutes.

Time that he has devoted to her, that he has entwined her within—and now this.

He has been aware of what she is doing for several weeks but is certain it began months earlier, probably when the man was still just a guinea pig whoring himself for insignificant amounts of money. Dracyev knew she would wander through the corridors and often speak with the lab rats as they waited for their prescribed experiments to begin, and he has tolerated, though never approved, of it.

He promised her more, promised her whatever she desired, and yet she would always return to the festering vagrants lined up outside the labs at the start of each week.

Why she had found particular interest in that one creature Dracyev didn't know. Didn't want to know.

What mattered was that the creature found an interest in Ylena.

For a man such as this, a simple death was too good for him.

So he has summoned Konstantin, telling him to come to his private lab immediately and, while awaiting the man's arrival, Dracyev retrieves a fresh vial from one of the storage boxes on his workbench.

He unzips himself and pees into the vial, then seals the lid. He wipes the glass down then places it into the inscription machine, waits for it to randomly generate a code number and etch it into the vial, then records the number in his log book.

Konstantin arrives moments later, and at first it looks to Dracyev as if the other man has turned himself inside out— his suit's dark red hue is a refraction of his soft innards, the creases and rumples are his veins and arteries. His shirt is black, the thin tie that lies atop it like a perfectly described trachea.

"Mr. Dracyev?"

"I have something I need you to do for me, Konstantin. Tomorrow night, there will be a man, he will bring this vial to you to be taken onto the mainland. I need you to get off the island tonight and wait for him there."

Kostantin has taken out a cigarillo and lit it. Dracyev watches the smoke unravel from the man's mouth and travel toward the ceiling of the lab where it merges with the muddy stains already there.

"If I'm going to leave the island, why don't I just take the vial?"

"Because he's fucking her," Dracyev said firmly.

"I don't . . . ?"

"I know it's him. I've seen them together. Watched them. I won't tolerate it any longer."

"So what's in the vial? Poison?"

"The vial is nothing. The vial will lead him to you. I want you to kill him for me, Konstantin." Dracyev is talking a language the man in red understands.

"Easily done. Even more easily done if you just give me his address and I go over there now."

"No," Dracyev snaps. "They'll know they can't get away with this indefinitely, that I'll find out. I think Ylena already suspects I know something. She's been talking about the mainland more recently, about moving the operation across there entirely, and I'm certain it is him who has been putting the ideas in her head."

Dracyev turns to Konstantin, fixes him with a cold and bloody stare.

"I want him to die within sight of his fucking prize. I want him to die with the mainland at his feet and I want him to know, in that last moment, that he will never see her again."

Konstantin rolls the cigarillo from one corner of his mouth to the other. "To clarify—you're going to tell this man to deliver this vial to the mainland and that, what, I'm the contact?"

Dracyev nods.

"And you want this guy taken out."

Another nod.

Konstantin breathes smoke out through his nostrils, tongues it as it moves through the air.

"So what's his name?" he asks.

CHAPTER FIFTY-TWO

Konstantin says, "So you must be Januscz, is that correct?"

Janusz glances at Katja, smiles, then looks back at Konstantin.

"Yes," he says proudly. "I am Januscz."

An expression flickers across Konstantin's face but it's too quick for either Katja or Januscz to decipher. The man in red holds up the vial, then opens his hand, letting it drop to the ground. It cracks upon impact and, just to make sure, he stamps on it, shattering it into dozen of tiny fragments.

Januscz stares down at the mess in disbelief, then at the man who has made it.

"What the fu—?"

His words are first cut off by the sight of a large, badly scuffed gun pointed at his head, and then by the impact of a bullet blasting through his forehead just above his eyes. There's a moment's delay, as if his body or perhaps even gravity hasn't quite realized what has happened, and then he crumples to the deck.

Katja jumps in shock, stumbling backward and away from the killer, and suddenly the moment from earlier that night when she found out what Januscz was going to do to her replays in her head. But this time, this time the shot was good—no doubt about it.

Her momentum carries her and without a thought she is running, just running, knowing that at any moment a bullet will rip through her and end this whole sorry mess, but it doesn't. She thinks she hears a shot, but it could just have been one of the workers slamming a door.

And that's when she sees him.

Nikolai.

For a brief moment her instinct is to halt, to get away from him because who knows what part he is playing in all this, but that quickly subsides when she sees the expression on his face, something that tells her she is wrong.

"Katja, where have you . . . ?"

She grabs him as she passes, pulls him past a pair of workers standing in a doorway that leads into the storage area, pushes him down the stairs ahead of her and slams the door shut. She works the locks to secure them and hears the workers mumbling something but ignores them.

"We need to hide, Nikolai!" she shouts at him as they enter the belly of the boat. At the far end they see the light spilling in from the deck and the loading crews beginning their work.

"What's going on?"

"It's a fucking set-up!" she cries. "The man in red, he's just shot Januscz and destroyed the vial!"

"Januscz? I thought he was . . ."

"Yeah, well, you're not the only one."

She's pushing her way through all the crates, looking for somewhere, somewhere safe, and she finds her guitar, picks it up.

A door overhead opens and they both spin around, ready for the impact of the man in red's shots but it's not red they see, it's orange, the orange of loading crews overalls, just a couple of workers coming, that's all.

"This way," Nikolai says, and leads her to the opposite side of the storage bay to a crate, the side of which he pulls open. It looks like it has come off with surprising ease until Katja notices the bent screws and dents in the sides that indicate the crate has already been opened.

She steps inside the container, cringing at the pungent smell that emerges from it, then freezes.

"Holy shit."

Nikolai chews his lip as he says, "I should probably have mentioned that before I opened the door."

Katja kneels down next to the body of Dracyev, his blood having soaked into the sacks and polystyrene blocks around him.

"What the fuck happened?"

"I shot him," Nikolai says. "Well . . . I didn't mean to. I mean . . . I didn't know it was him—you know, Dracyev."

"He found you?"

"Not exactly. He was talking to someone. He had a gun. I just . . . reacted."

"Who was he talking to?"

"I don't know, some guy and a woman. They ran off after I shot Dracyev."

Katja shakes her head. "This just keeps getting better and better."

The sounds of the loaders is getting closer; they're reeling off code numbers to each other one by one as the cranes haul crates out of the storage area and into the night air, ready to be lowered onto the docks. Great chains rattle and scrape against one another, the whine of a winch rising in pitch then falling again. The thud of wood on metal echoes around them.

"Get in," she says, and they both duck inside the crate, in with Dracyev's body and his sticky blood.

She pulls the side of the crate shut after them, jerking it hard enough to impale the soft wood on the bent nails. She lets go gently and is relieved to see that it holds, though there is a small crack of light at the bottom left-hand corner.

They both retreat to the back of the crate, trying to avoid Dracyev's body where possible.

"What's going on?" Nikolai whispers.

"I don't know. Either it's a set-up or Januscz has been up to something bigger than I first realized. Perhaps he wasn't meant to have the vial after all, I don't know."

"He stole it?"

"I don't know, Nikolai."

"Where's the vial?"

"The vial's gone, destroyed."

"But . . ."

"Look," Katja snaps, and has to force herself to be quiet again. "The one thing I *do* know right now is that there is a killer up there and he's just shot Januscz and he's probably coming after me next, and if you don't shut the fuck up he's going to fucking well find us!"

Nikolai swallows the chunk of nail he's just bitten off and it catches in his throat.

"What happened to your face?" he asks.

"Nikolai, shut the fuck—!"

And she stops speaking abruptly, stiffens.

Shuffling outside.

A shape flashes across the gap, then returns.

Katja hears the man's hands running across the wood, exploring it. She feels something touch her and turns and it's Nikolai, he's holding a gun out to her. The end of the weapon is crusted with blood but she's lost track of whose it might be. She takes it, aims it at the crack and Nikolai mirrors her with another weapon.

The crate creaks as someone leans against it, and a hand becomes visible.

CHAPTER FIFTY-THREE

He pulls on his heavy-duty gloves and follows the others up the loading ramp, just one of many workers about to start their shift.

But he doesn't line up with the others, to wait until the cranes are ready to begin as he normally would. This time he strides right past them, his attention briefly grabbed by a man in a red suit tipping a body over the edge of the boat, and he knows who the man works for so keeps going, keeps walking until he reaches the doors that lead into the storage bay below.

Another worker is already there and holds open the door for him. Smiles are exchanged.

He goes down the steps, then pulls back his glove to reveal the number etched there. This is the number he had been given earlier that night by his colleague on the island, the number that lead to the promise of more cash than he could expect in a month with his regular wages.

He walks amongst the crates, scanning the numbers stamped onto them as he finally finds the one he is looking for. One of the sides has been crow-barred open and then closed awkwardly again, leaving a slight gap down one side. He mutters a criticism about his fellow conspirator's sloppy work, gives the wood a shove and impales it further on the nails until the gap is closed.

He checks that no one is looking, then reaches up and runs his hand along the top until he touches something small and plastic. He pulls it down and looks inside, breaks a smile when he sees the thick blocks of notes.

"You need a hand there?"

One of the other workers, hands on his hips.

"No, it's fine. I've got this one."

CHAPTER FIFTY-FOUR

Shit, we're moving," Katja says, gun still pointed ahead of her into the darkness, waiting for the assassin that so far hasn't come.

The crate creaks from the strain, the sound vibrating around them and they are thrown to one side suddenly, then back again. Dracyev's body slides along beneath them, greased by his own blood, nestles up against the far edge.

Katja and Nikolai both crouch down, lowering their centre of gravity and steadying their balance. Machine sounds fill the hot, carbon-heavy air around them, and all they can do is hold on.

"It's him," Nikolai murmurs, squeezing himself into a corner. "It's the man in red, he knows we're in here."

"Nikolai, shut up."

"He's going to dump us in the fucking water!" he shouts.

"Shut up!" Katja barks back, then feels her stomach suddenly sink as she considers that he might be right.

The rattling continues, the sudden shifts from side to side, the mechanical grinding and the call of gulls, the sounds of the ocean and the thoughts of *it can't end like this*, the irony that death will deliver them pre-packaged for burial even if it is just at the bottom of the sea.

They hear the barked instructions of the loaders, the whine of pulleys and then it all fades and there is an almighty thump that throws them forward and through Dracyev's sticky blood. Nikolai becomes entangled in the body, scrabbling to get out from under a wet, rapidly cooling limb, and Katja snaps at him.

"Shhhhh!"

The noises have stopped, fallen away to an even more worrying silence.

They hear footsteps, draw their guns again, but then realize the footsteps are fading away. Someone is walking away.

And they wait there, interminably, guns aimed at where they think the man in red might appear, until their arms are too heavy and they have to let them drop.

Nikolai looks at Katja.

Katja looks at Nikolai.

Waiting for the other to move, to react.

"Fuck this, I'm not sitting here waiting to die," she says, and just strides across to the side that had been opened before and boots it hard at the join, and Nikolai shouts for her to stop, and the crate bursts open and they both brace themselves.

Nothing.

Silence.

Dusty darkness, like the inside of a garage.

Or the inside of a warehouse.

Katja checks the immediate area but it's clear. There's nobody there.

There are a handful of other crates that look like they've been there for years, old rusted chains scattered across the ground, graffiti on the walls. And windows above a steel-fronted doorway.

"Well . . . ?" Nikolai asks from within the crate.

Katja turns to him, shakes her head. Shrugs.

He follows her out cautiously and the gun, he's forgotten about it, it's hanging loosely by his side like a numbed limb.

Katja walks over to the warehouse's main door, guitar once again slung across her back, the neck now broken and only held together by a single fret. She hauls herself up onto a pipe that runs parallel to the ground and balances so she can see out of the greasy windows above. She cups a hand over her eyes to get a better view.

"Do you see them?" Nikolai asks.

"I see the loading crews," she tells him. "We must be on the mainland."

A pause, she wipes the muck from the window, then, "Fuck, Nikolai."

"What?"

She looks down at him, her swollen face—somehow still pretty—gleaming in the light that bathes her.

"The boat. It's gone."

She drops down and walks toward the opposite side of the small warehouse, finds another, smaller doorway. She raises her gun and reaches for the handle, turns it.

The door opens and she peers out.

She sees the carcasses of other warehouses scattered around before her, the veins of alleyways formed by the tight spaces between them.

And nobody around.

She steps outside in the way you would in a dream, not quite sure of the laws that now govern you, if they reflect the real world or repel it. And with each step she takes, those laws return, solidify, and she realizes that everything is the way it should be.

They are on the mainland.

The man in red is gone.

Dracyev is dead.

Januscz is dead.

Kohl is dead.

"We're here," she says, as much to herself as to Nikolai. "We're fucking here."

CHAPTER FIFTY-FIVE

So they're on the mainland and they are suddenly aware that everything's cool. That they just might have made it and are free.

From the island.

From Januscz.

From Aleksakhina, from the arcades, and perhaps even from the drugs.

Perhaps.

They've made their way through the network of alleyways, away from the docks and out toward the city beyond. They stop at the edge of a highway that spirals up along the coasts and into the distance. They're high enough now to see over the storage buildings and across the water and the island which glitters there in the distance.

"It looks a lot more peaceful from over here, doesn't

it?" Katja says. The right side of her face has gone numb and she's grateful for it. Nikolai's sense of balance and orientation has just about fully returned.

They both stand at the edge of the road, dust blasting into their faces as a truck shoots past, trailing a visual ribbon of red brake light behind it. They watch it until it disappears over a hill in the distance, then everything is quiet and it's just them.

So far everything has been about getting off the island, getting to the mainland; there has been nothing else to think about beyond that.

But what now?

In the near distance they see the lights of a diner, broken neon signage flickering in the darkness.

"You hungry?" Katja asks.

"I guess so."

"You want to grab something to eat?"

"Sure."

"It'll make a change to be served instead of having to do the serving. You got any money?"

"Erm . . ."

"Me neither." She shrugs, continues toward the diner. "I guess we'll figure something out."

"Yeah."

"What about your guitar?"

Katja swings the instrument around from her back. The neck is hanging on by the merest thread of splintered wood now, the fret holding it in place bent out of shape and looking as if it's going to snap.

"Shit, man. I've had this thing for years."

"Maybe we can get it repaired."

"Yeah, maybe."

"You know anybody on the mainland?"

"No—you?"

Nikolai shakes his head.

"Don't worry about it. We'll soon find somewhere to hook up. I'll check out the punk scene, see what's going on. There's always something there."

Nikolai nods, and something about the way he does it makes Katja think of the kid who's left over once the teams have been picked for a neighbourhood game of basketball.

"You might as well stick with me," she says as they reach the gravel entrance to the diner.

Nikolai doesn't say anything, just chews on a nail.

And as she pushes open the door to the diner, she asks him, "So you play any instruments, Nikolai?"

He shakes his head, mumbles something about his fingers being too screwed up from the arcade machines, and they sit together in a booth near the back.

"Doesn't matter," she tells him, nodding for one of the waitresses. "If you're not musical, you could always just be a drummer."

"I don't really know . . ."

"Two coffees, please," she says to the tall brunette now looming over them. "And you'd better bring more sugar."

". . . how to play," Nikolai finishes.

To the waitress, "Thanks," and to Nikolai, "Play? Shit, man, you don't have to know how to play—it's drumming, any idiot can do it."

And Nikolai sort of smiles as he tries to figure out if there is a compliment in there somewhere.

"If nobody's looking, then we'll just start our own band. That'll get us some money, short-term. After that . . ."

The coffee arrives and Nikolai is looking at her expectantly, steam rising from the mug beneath him.

Katja shrugs. "After that, we'll figure it out. We can do whatever the fuck we want over here, go wherever the fuck we want, do you realize that?"

"I gue—"

"No dickhead boyfriends, no parole officers trailing my ass around day and night, no fucking idiot bosses telling me what to do. It's a new start—for you as well."

Nikolai heaps sugar into his coffee, sips until he feels the familiar sting on his teeth. "Yeah."

"Things are going to work out for us now, Nikolai, you know? For too fucking long we've both been getting fucked over by everyone around us. It's time for things to change."

And Nikolai, he's looking at the two games machines in the very corner of the diner next to the toilets, focusing on their flickering lights and the pixel-music, trying to suppress the growing fire in his gut. He's thinking that not everything has been left behind on the island, that some things you just can't change. You just can't get rid of.

But Katja has got him this far.

She's done what everyone on the island thought impossible—escape—and maybe she's right, maybe things can start anew. Maybe he really can leave it all behind.

He looks at her slumped in the booth across from him, her liberty spikes broken and flopping across her shoulders, her lip ring and trach tubing glittering in the overhead lighting, this woman—his supposed saviour.

He swallows the rest of the coffee in one gulp, the dregs of sugar at the bottom pouring into his mouth like sand from an hourglass, and he has to squeeze them down his throat.

"So you want to split now or what?" she asks him.

"Sure, I . . . what about the . . . ?"

And she puts a finger to her lips to silence him, glances over her shoulder at the waitress.

"Wait until she's serving those guys over there. I heard them order two chilis so her hands will be full. As soon as you see her come out from the kitchen, make a run for the door."

"I . . . but . . ."

"Okay, go . . ."

And Katja gets up swiftly from the booth, sliding her way out, grabbing her guitar, and she's striding toward the door, head low, and just then the waitress is coming out from the kitchen, a bowl of chili in each hand and she sees the punk leaving, shouts, "Hey!" but Katja is gone, the door slamming shut behind her.

The waitress's attention switches to Nikolai and panic hits him and he jerks upright, clattering his knees off the booth and stumbling out into another table, struggling to regain his balance, and he's chasing after Katja yet again and he was right, he realizes—he was right.

Some things you just can't change.

ABOUT THE AUTHOR

SIMON LOGAN

Simon Logan is the author of the industrial fiction novel *Pretty Little Things To Fill Up The Void*, the industrial short story collections *I-O* and *Nothing Is Inflammable*, and the fetishcore collection *Rohypnol Brides*. He can reached through his website: www.coldandalone.com